Case of the Bedevilled Poet

Case of the Bedevilled Poet

A Sherlock Holmes Enigma

Simon Clark

NewCon Press
England

First published in the UK by NewCon Press
41 Wheatsheaf Road, Alconbury Weston, Cambs, PE28 4LF
June 2017

NCP 123 (limited edition hardback)
NCP 124 (softback)

10 9 8 7 6 5 4 3 2 1

ISBN:

978-1-910935-47-7 (hardback)
978-1-910935-48-4 (softback)

Cover art by Vincent Sammy
Cover layout by Andy Bigwood

Minor editorial meddling by Ian Whates
Book layout by Storm Constantine

Simon Clark

One of a Special Edition, Signed by the Author
Limited to just 100 numbered copies
This is number:

53

1. London's Burning Heart

Jack Crofton stood watching the newspaper offices go up in flames. Two hours ago, Nazi war planes had rained bombs from the night sky onto Fleet Street.

His friend, Bill Tulley, took a slug of whisky from his hipflask. "The whole bloody place is going up. The sky's black with smoke."

Jack eyed the hipflask, wishing Bill would offer him a drink of that wonderful warming spirit. "The printing machines are burning," he murmured. "Ink-black smoke. Blacker than the darkness in the hearts of Man."

"Blacker than Hades."

"You're drunk."

"So are you."

Jack Crofton's eyes were fixed on the shining, beautiful, hipflask, not the hundred- year-old structure that screamed, or so it sounded to his ears, as ruptured gas pipes jetted flames with the power of blow-torches.

Bill nodded at the ruined newspaper building. "That's the end of *The Times*."

"It's the end of all times," Jack pointed out. "London's been bombed for the tenth night in a row."

A fire engine rumbled up behind them. One of the firemen, standing on the running board fixed to the side of the vehicle, waved his arm, shooing Jack and Bill aside. "Get out of the way!

Bloody fools."

Bill lurched forwards. "We're not bloody fools! I'm an artist. My friend here, Mr Crofton, is a poet!"

The clanging of the fire engine bell drowned Bill's riposte. The vehicle weaved around the pair in the street in order to continue on its way to the inferno. Jack needed whisky. Earlier that evening he'd downed five pints of pale ale; however, the warmth and charm, and Dutch courage, the beer had bestowed upon him receded, allowing reality – cold, unwelcome reality to intrude.

Jack said, "Bill, give me some whisky."

Bill Tulley didn't hear. That strapping thirty-four-year-old man, in gold-framed glasses, and sporting a soft velvet cap, which he insisted all creative people should wear to warm the blood flowing around the brain, swayed. Clearly, the whisky was stealing away his sense of balance. His eyes gleamed as he watched all the activity with drunken fascination. Firemen began unrolling hoses. Police constables gestured to sightseers to keep back. A man of around sixty in a white helmet hurried toward Jack and Bill, his face flushed, eyes glittering. The ARP lettering on the front of the helmet marked him out as a civilian who'd volunteered to patrol the streets to advise people when the air-raid warning sounded; additionally, he would make sure no lights could be seen in buildings that would guide enemy bomber pilots to their targets.

The ARP man called out, "Hey, you two – you should be in a shelter. There's an unexploded bomb in The Wheatsheaf!"

"The Wheatsheaf?" Bill swayed. "We won't be drinking there tonight."

"Picture the bomb." Jack closed his eyes. "Iron cylinder. Fins A detonator, and an explosive heart – the metal beast lurks in the tavern. All those bottles of whisky lying broken on the floor. A pool – no, an entire lagoon of gorgeous spirit evaporating into Godless, Godforsaken air."

"Now that's a tragedy." Bill pushed the neck of the hipflask between his lips in order to take a long hard swallow before uttering, "A real wartime tragedy."

An ambulance dashed by. Blood trickled from beneath its back doors, leaving crimson spots the size of pennies in a long line down the street.

Then the breeze turned around. Clouds of vile smelling smoke that seemed to possess teeth that bit the back of Jack's throat rolled over him.

"You know." Bill coughed. "I've not said anything until now. But I'm standing on a man's face. Just a face, with a beard and nothing else."

Fifty yards away the front of the building collapsed with a thundering roar. The wall had been holding the heat back. Now a tidal wave of hot air scorched Jack's face. The smoke tore into his lungs. He retreated into an alleyway, coughing, spluttering.

"Bill…" Blinded by fumes and heat, he reached out for his friend. "Bill…"

"I'm not Bill. Get your hands off me."

Jack rubbed his stinging eyes. There, in front of him, loomed a soldier. A wounded soldier – with a great, slashing cut across his face, stitched with black thread forming a line of crosses: xxxx. Jack turned around. No sign of his friend Bill. He was alone with the man who wore a torn, dirty uniform – a corporal's stripes decorated one arm. The man's brown eyes were narrow, hating. He clearly didn't like the look of Jack Crofton who'd stumbled into the alleyway, perhaps a place that the infantryman considered to be his personal domain.

Jack muttered, "I'm sorry."

"I bet you are." The soldier lit a cigarette. He made the action of holding the burning match to its tip and sucking in the smoke aggressive, and deeply ominous, as if he'd lit a fuse to the explosive anger inside of him. "What's your name?" he demanded.

"Jack Crofton."

"Rank?"

"No rank. Don't have one. I'm not in the armed services."

"I thought not."

"I'm on my way home."

"Like being at home, do you? Cosy, is it? Too cosy to go fight in the war?"

"I'm in a reserved occupation." Jack noticed the tremor in his own voice the same time he noticed the soldier bunch his hands into hard-looking fists. "I'm serving the war effort."

"Reserved occupation. That's another word for 'coward'. Have you ever been in uniform?"

"No."

"What do you do, then?"

"Write scripts."

"Scripts. What are they?"

The soldier stood with his face just inches from Jack's own. Blue tobacco smoke jetted from the man's nostrils. The xxxx line of stitches pulled tight when he scowled, and the lips of the wound that ran from the bottom of his left eye to his top lip tightened as well, as if forming a deeply unsettling grimace.

"Scripts…" Jack began, now stone cold sober through sheer fright, "…scripts are a story written down on paper which is then made into a film."

"And that's you helping us win the war against, Hitler? Making up stories."

"People see films in the cinema. It makes them feel better in themselves. Hopeful."

The soldier's lips slid back to expose yellow teeth. "You know what, mate?" He jabbed his finger into Jack's chest. "You're a coward. You stay at home, poncing about with a pen and paper, writing bloody yarns, when people like me are being killed for King and Country."

"I'm not. I –"

"I'll give you reserved occupation, you little smear of shit."

The solider pushed Jack against the wall. The man's strength was immense. Jack's head whipped back, smashing against the bricks. He grunted with pain.

The soldier stepped forward through the gloom. The light from the blazing newspaper offices fell directly onto his face; the man's eyes looked as if they'd been replaced with balls of yellow flame.

The man flung the cigarette aside. "I'm going to be your own personal monster. I'm going to make you suffer." Beads of crimson oozed from the wound to trickle down his cheek. "And suffer you shall before you die."

He swung a punch at Jack's head. Jack raised his arm in time to stop the blow with his forearm. Even so, that punch felt as if a hammer had struck the limb. He yelped.

Once again, the soldier drew back his fist, ready to deliver a punch that would, Jack knew, transform his face into a mangled ruin. Another ambulance roared by the end of the alleyway, bell ringing. The soldier glanced in its direction for a split-second. That was enough time for Jack to run. He raced down the alley from Fleet Street in the direction of the River Thames. Street lights had been turned off to maintain a blackout in the hope enemy bombers wouldn't find London in the dark. The lack of light also meant that Jack ran in near-darkness, his hand out in front of him, as he tried to make out the dim cliffs at either side, which were the rear portions of monumental buildings.

His attacker followed, heavy boots smashing against the ground with a sound like gunfire. Jack knew he'd be beaten bloody if the man caught him. Even as he ran, he turned back time inside his head, hoping that he'd un-meet the angry soldier in the alley: a man with a vengeful hatred of stay-at-home cowards. In Jack's imagination, time continued to flow backwards. Now in his mind's eye he could see himself standing with his friend Bill Tulley, watching the building blaze in reverse, until the bomb soared (intact, unexploded) back up into the sky to slip inside the plane. Then, eventually, he'd be travelling on a backwards running train to Yorkshire, to return to his father on the station platform, who would utter, "All that time you wanted to be a poet, and your mother pushing me to let you stay at home and bloody scribble in your book all day. Now, instead of joining the army and making us proud by being a fighting man, you're running away to London to bring shame on your family. Fooling around with stuff for picture houses."

But Jack couldn't turn back time. The soldier chased him. Jack would have his nose broken, his teeth shattered. Pain would be his bedfellow tonight. He turned a corner so quickly that he slipped. The next thing he knew he was sliding face-down across the ground, stone cobbles bumping against his chin. Running footsteps got louder. Any second the furious stranger would crash around the corner to find him.

Then, there in the gloom, he made out steps leading down to a basement. Sound came through a door. Music, muffled voices. Jack scrambled to his feet before half-falling, half running down the steps. Then he was through the door into a corridor with plush carpets. Posters on the walls were covered with French slogans garlanding pictures of half-naked women.

A notice on a door warned:

Private
Cinema
Members Only

He was alone in the corridor. His heart leapt as he recognized an opportunity to save himself. Within seconds he was through the door into a gloomy room with rows of seats and a screen at the far end, where silvery images danced before a dozen or so men sitting with their trilbies on their laps. Cigar smoke painted the air blue.

Jack ducked his head and dropped into a seat.

For a long time he sat there, eyes fixed on the door he'd come through. At any moment, the soldier would step through. See him. Then fists would rain down. Jack saw himself screaming in agony as hard knuckles bruised his face.

Long moments crept by – slowly, painfully.

No soldier appeared. Jack sighed with relief. He'd given the man the slip.

Jack turned his face back to the screen. He realised he was now watching a newsreel that included some story or other about Nazi propaganda minister, Joseph Goebbels. The man's narrow face, studded with a pair of tiny eyes filled the screen. He'd been talking to a platoon of Stormtroopers in German, then, strangely – impossibly – Goebbels noticed Jack in the cinema audience.

Goebbels glared at Jack. Then he spoke in English: "I'm going to be your own personal monster. I'm going to make you suffer." The Nazi bigwig nodded with satisfaction. "And suffer you shall before you die."

Jack realised he walked along a narrow street. He didn't know how he'd got there. His heart thudded painfully, telling him he must have been running. Sweat trickled down his back, making his skin itch unpleasantly.

A boy of about fourteen leaned out of a downstairs window just five feet from him.

The lad hissed: "I'm going to be your own personal monster. I'm going to make you suffer. And suffer you shall before you die."

That was the moment Jack realised a monster had invaded his life. A monster that had embarked on a quest to inflict pain. To terrorise. And, ultimately, aim to kill him.

Moments later, Jack met a policeman cycling toward him. The copper pedalled along an otherwise deserted street with ponderous solemnity.

Jack ran toward him. "Constable, my life has been threatened."

"I'm off duty."

"Didn't you hear? Someone wants to kill me."

"Go home, lad, your drunk."

"I'm not."

The policeman pedalled by. "I can smell ale from here."

"You've got to help me."

"Look, just sod off, or you'll get my boot up your backside."

The policeman glided away into darkness. Jack headed in the other direction, feeling panicky; expecting a figure to leap from the shadows to attack him. The first pub he reached he dived in without hesitation and ordered a double whisky. He downed the fiery liquor straight away; he ordered another, and another...

The pub landlord, a large man with one eye, his face as red as a strawberry, matched him drink for drink. There were half a dozen customers in the bar – mainly older men in flat caps, smoking cigarettes and supping pints of lukewarm brown ale. An RAF man in a blue uniform sat with a woman in a small lounge off the main bar. Jack edged further along the counter to make sure he'd be out of sight of the fly boy.

When he bought another whisky he confided in the landlord, "I've been threatened tonight. Someone wants to kill me."

"You don't say." The landlord moved away into a back room of the pub.

Jack shuffled toward a man in a long coat and flat cap who stood at the end of the bar. A black Labrador sat at the man's feet. The dog held a piece of raw meat in its jaws.

"It's not right, is it?" Jack said. Fright had turned into an aching sense of injustice that the whisky couldn't ease. "There I am, minding my own business."

"Like I'm minding mine." The man sipped his beer.

"Out of nowhere comes this brute. He actually thinks he has the legal right to assault me and – and threaten to make me suffer."

"And suffer you shall before you die."

Jack took a step back, gulping with shock. "What did you just say?"

"I'm just here for a quiet drink. I don't want bothering."

Jack retreated into another section of the bar where the lights were little more than a dim glow. His heart pounded; he was panting with fear. The only other people in this corner of the pub were two men of around seventy. They sat to a small table, face-to-face, as if they'd been swapping secrets. One had a round, pink face with a thick moustache. The other man's face was thin… no, more than thin. The face was gaunt to the point where the skin only just managed to cover the skull without tearing.

The two men broke off their furtive whispering to look Jack up and down.

"What do you make of him?" asked the gaunt man.

"Agitated, I'd say," answered the round-faced man. "Probably caught up in the blitz. Run ragged by fright."

"He's afraid. Even terrified. But, no — not due to the fear of falling bombs. The man is scared because he's been hunted as you'd hunt a wild animal. He's been running for his life. And now he's looking for a place to hide." The gaunt man's sharp eyes seemed to penetrate Jack's face, searching inside his head, looking for clues. "Am I on the right track, sir?"

"Yes, you are." Jack's stared at the thin man in surprise.

"Just as I thought."

Jack took a step forward, his entire body trembling with relief at not being ignored or turned away. "I need help. You see, men have threatened me."

The round-faced man shook his head in sympathy. "Shocking state-of-affairs."

The gaunt one touched the back of an empty chair. "Sit down. Tell us what happened."

Jack felt a surge of gratitude. "Who are you?"

The man, who'd invited him to sit, pointed a very thin finger at his well-built friend. "This is Doctor Watson. And I'm Sherlock Holmes."

2. The Case of the Fearful Writer

A typewriter rattled furiously in the next room. Ivy Lee would be typing new contracts for the staff at Sagenta Studios. These were the military-exempt folk, who worked on patriotic films funded by the government. Pay was good – much, much higher than Jack Crofton was accustomed to as a thirty-three year old poet with only one skinny-thin collection of verse to his name.

Jack listened to Ivy's lightning-fast typing, visualising his name appearing in capitals at the top of the contract: *This contract is made the twentieth day of November, 1944, between JACK CROFTON (hereinafter known as 'the Writer') and SAGENTA STUDIOS LIMITED...*

Picturing his name there on the document, even though he hadn't been informed that his services would still be required at the start of 1945, gave Jack a reassuring warmth, powerful enough to make him forget the devil of a hangover he's woken up with that morning, or the inexplicable bruising on one arm. He rolled a sheet of paper into the typewriter on his desk, and typed: -

<u>HEY, MATE, DON'T BLAME THE GENERAL</u>
<u>Script by Jack Crofton</u>
Film duration: 10 minutes

Purpose of story: to discourage military personnel from criticising superior officers, which leads to discontent and low morale amongst the ranks.

Jack leant back in the chair before reaching into his jacket pocket for his smokes. When he pulled out the pack he saw an address scribbled on a piece of paper tucked between the two remaining cigarettes. As he read the address: 11E Merchant Terrace, Fitzrovia, memories came flooding back of the previous evening: watching the newspaper building going up in flames, then being chased by the soldier, before eventually finding his way to a small tavern where he met –

"Sherlock Holmes and Doctor Watson. Dear God... I was drunk as the proverbial parasite in ermine." He rubbed his forehead as the hangover renewed its vicious attack on his skull.

Until seeing that shred of paper just now, bearing the unfamiliar scribble, he'd dismissed the bizarre encounter with the two men as a dream. Also, recalling the two oddballs, who claimed to be the legendary Holmes and Watson, prompted him to remember the nightmarish threats uttered by the soldier and the boy: "I am your personal monster." Or words to that effect.

"I was really drunk," Jack muttered by way of shining a rational light onto the irrational horror of last night.

He lit a cigarette and closed his eyes. Now he found that he could conjure vivid memories of sitting with the two men – both in their seventies, he guessed; one so gaunt that the skin seemed to have been painted thinly over the front of his skull. The other man: plump, red cheeked, with a bulbous boozer's nose. After he'd bought the two men a whisky apiece they'd carefully listened to his story of being threatened by strangers – and also that impossible threat by Doctor Goebbels from the cinema screen.

The man claiming to be Sherlock Holmes had declared grandly, "I shall take your case. There will be a fee payable to myself, of course."

"I don't have much money," Jack had answered.

Doctor Watson, if that was his real name, had a compromise. "Come to this flat tomorrow evening at seven." He'd then written the Merchant Terrace address on a scrap of paper which he handed to Jack. "Bring a bottle of Scotch by way of down payment. We'll conduct a detailed interview with you."

Holmes steepled his fingers together. "In order to identify cogent facts that might have a bearing on your case."

"The case of the fearful writer," Watson added with a cheerful smile.

In the cold light of day, with nothing remaining of his drunken evening but a dry-mouth, and skull-needling hangover, Jack realised that he'd been taken for a ride. In every pub you'll always find strangers who are friendly and interested in what you have to say, providing you keep buying them drinks. The two fakers, pretending to be the world-famous detective and his side-kick, were clearly only interested in the glasses of Johnnie Walker that Jack was providing. They were no more crime-fighting geniuses than he was.

Jack dropped the scrap of paper, bearing the address, into the rubbish basket next to his desk.

At that moment, Frankie, the office boy, breezed into the room with a bright, cheery, "Henley Woolworth's got blitzed last night. There's nothing but a big hole in the ground. Water's gushing up from the mains supply as high as the church tower."

Jack tapped ash from his cigarette into a tea cup. "*The Times* offices bought it, too."

"Didn't they print one of your poems?"

"Aye. First time I got decent money for one as well."

Frankie wore a yellow checked jacket and green knitted tie. He wanted to become an actor. He'd taken the job as office boy at the studio in the hope they'd put him in front of the cameras one day. Jack liked the boy. His naïve optimism reminded Jack of all those evenings he spent in his bedroom, when he lived with his parents, writing pages of verse, dreaming of becoming a famous poet one day, when he'd drink beer in pubs with his hero Dylan

Thomas, and they'd paint the town red, and be applauded by adoring audiences when they gave readings in the Albert Hall. Jack had only met Dylan Thomas once at a publisher's party.

Dylan Thomas had confided: "When I was fifteen I detested the taste of beer. Now I detest everything that does not taste of beer." By the time of that meeting, Thomas, son of a Swansea schoolteacher, had made a reputation for himself as a famous poet, appearing in print as well as reciting his verse on the radio. During the party, the Welsh bard had borrowed ten shillings from Jack, saying "I'll pay you back on Monday. The BBC is sending me a juicy, ripe cheque, dripping with pound signs." That was six months ago. Jack hadn't clapped eyes on Thomas since. As for the ten shillings... well, Thomas had also developed a certain reputation when it came to repaying debts. That is to say, he never ever did.

Frankie sat in a swivel chair next to Jack and spun round and around, his legs stretching out, knocking the wastepaper basket flying, scattering fag ends and balls of paper.

"Mrs Mercer sent me to tell you that one of the actresses hasn't turned up."

"Rowena?"

"Nah, the one who plays tea lady."

"We're filming the factory scene this morning. The tea lady's in that."

Frankie stopped spinning. "God, that makes you dizzy." He jiggled his head to ease the vertigo. "Mrs Mercer says you need to rewrite the scene so Rowena can play it by herself. You know... monologue?"

"I've got to see Jensen at ten."

"Uh?" Frankie glanced at his watch. "It's already five minutes past."

"Damn." Jumping out of the chair, Jack dunked the cigarette into a tea cup. "Tell Mrs Mercer I'll be down in the studio in ten minutes."

"Aye, aye, chief."

19

As Jack hurried out of the room Frankie started spinning again.

Jack knocked on a door at the end of the passageway.

Straight away, he heard a curt, "Come."

He entered the plush office that smelt strongly of its leather sofa and Jensen's cigars.

"Ten, wasn't it, Crofton?"

"Sorry, sir, the director needs me to rewrite a scene she's shooting this morning."

Jensen, a small, waspish man, with black hair so shiny that each strand looked as if it had been rinsed in olive oil, remained seated behind a vast oak desk. Nor did he invite Jack to sit. Oliver Jensen owned the studio. Although he described himself as a film producer, he mainly concentrated on the financial aspects of the picture industry. Jensen drove a Rolls Royce. Rumour had it that his house boasted a private cinema.

"Well?" asked Jensen through clouds of richly aromatic tobacco smoke.

"I'd like to expand the final scene in *The C-Clip Girls*."

"Expand? Sounds expensive."

"At the moment, it's not very dramatic. In fact, something of an anti-climax."

"Go on."

"The object of the film is to demonstrate that the work of factory girls is vital to the war effort. We illustrate this by showing one such factory girl drilling holes into C-Clips all day. The C-Clip is a component of a machine gun-"

"Yes, yes, I get that. The C-Clip, I believe, is... What is it now? Ah, a newly-invented part of the firing mechanism that stops the gun from jamming."

"Which will save the lives of our fighting men. After all, a gun that's jammed can't fire bullets."

"So, why change the end of the film?"

"At the climax, we have the navigator in one of our aircraft firing the machine gun at the Nazi bomber which then blows up."

"Yes. Perfect."

"But just firing the gun isn't that dramatic. I was thinking Hitler and Mussolini could appear in demon-form in the RAF plane and try to make the gun jam. They can't because of the C-Clip in the mechanism." Oliver Jenner's blank expression made Jack talk faster as nervousness took hold. He detested trying to convey story concepts to his boss. He felt like a dim-witted school boy being given a mental arithmetic test in front of the entire class. Jack hated mental arithmetic, too. "So... Hitler and Mussolini reach into the machine gun with ghostly hands that we see through. They're pulling at the C-Clip while saying, 'I don't understand why the British gun does not jam. What is this component that makes the gun keep firing?' Then Hitler erupts into a screaming rage demanding to know why the British can manufacture the perfect machine gun that-"

Jenner held up his hand. "How do Hitler and Mussolini board a plane that's flying through the air?"

"They're not real. They look like ghosts."

"And they can fly?"

"No, they just appear in the plane."

Jenner tapped a leather-bound leger on his desk. "All the costings for the film have been finalised. There is no more money in the budget for your Hitler and Mussolini."

"Without them attacking the machine gun, there is no real jeopardy"

"Jeopardy?"

"Yes, if we revise the ending, the audience will be in suspense, wondering if these demon-beings will stop the gun from firing. Because if the gun fails the enemy plane will drop its bombs on the hospital. Everyone will be killed."

Jenner's forehead creased as he thought about what he'd just heard, then the skin smoothed out when he smiled. "I know how to make it more exciting. Have the plane lurch. The gunner can fall back into the... the plane's inner machinery, or whatever's in there, and he has to claw his way out before he can fire the gun again, destroy the enemy plane, and save everyone. Yes, that will do it, Crofton. Write that into the script. The gunner falls. Become stuck, etcetera, etcetera."

Thanking the man politely, Jack left the office, red-faced with embarrassment, wishing he'd never tried to make the film even remotely interesting. After all, these propaganda shorts were shown before the main feature at the cinema. Very few people in the audience would actually enjoy them.

Jack crossed the yard from the office building to the big tin shed that formed the studio. A blackboard hung beside the door. Chalked on the blackboard were the words: SILENCE PLEASE! WE ARE FILMING! 'C-CLIP GIRLS'. DIRECTOR: MEG MERCER.

He walked through heavy rubber flaps into the studio. Lights blazed down onto the set, which consisted of factory machines, including a work bench where an actress stood – her face painted stark white, with dark red lips, and striking black eye make-up; all of which would make the face appear luminously beautiful on screen. In real life, the make-up transformed her face into a strange mask. *A face like death itself,* thought Jack.

Technicians attached a sealed container, roughly a figure of eight shape, to the camera. This held the sixteen millimetre film. The lighting rig filled the studio with the odour of what Jack thought of as hot, raw electricity – an acrid, burning smell. The sound man swung a long pole across, from which the microphone hung, until the device was just above the actresses' head.

Jack nodded at her. "Hello, Rowena."

She smiled back. Two months ago, he'd eventually mustered the courage to ask her to go to the pictures with him. He'd joked, 'Knowing our luck, we'll end up seeing one of our own rotten films'. She'd ticked him off, sternly pointing out they were part of the war effort, keeping up public morale.

Pissing into the wind, more like, he'd thought sourly. But he didn't say the words out loud. He liked Rowena a lot. In a casual, non-committed way, they'd become boyfriend and girlfriend, though not lovers yet. Jack had suffered torments of self-doubt as he fell completely and utterly in love with her, because he did not know if she felt the same way about him. When she smiled his heart would start to pound, and even now, when sober, he felt absurdly shy. Even speaking full sentences to her became profoundly difficult.

He said, "I hear that, well… the tea lady…" He wanted to bite his own tongue until it hurt. What he'd just mumbled at her sounded stupidly inarticulate.

Rowena didn't appear to notice. She gave a wonderful smile with those red lips that were so breathtakingly striking. "Oh, the actress playing her is stuck in Brighton. There's an unexploded bomb on the railway line." She smoothed down the blue boiler suit she wore to create the factory worker look. However, her blond hair had been carefully brushed and fluffed around her head to inject glamour into a story about seemingly ordinary factory girls – studios were instructed by the Ministry of Information not to make actors overly dowdy and prosaic. This was wartime. Cinema audiences should be offered at least a small measure of escapism.

The director appeared from a small side office.

"Jack." She strode forward in her smart two-piece suit of jacket and narrow pencil skirt. "You know we've lost our tea lady?"

"Stranded in Brighton," Jack said as Rowena shot him a lovely smile before sitting in a chair so the make-up girl could touch up her lipstick.

Meg Mercer turned over pages of script until she found the scene they were filming. "Rowena is supposed to have a conversation with the tea lady. Now that nicely informative chat will have to be a monologue. Any ideas?"

Jack said, "She can't just spout about the importance of making the C-Clip into thin air."

"Agreed." Meg pulled a pencil from behind her ear. "I thought of shots of Rowena drilling holes into the clip blanks, then adding her voice-over later."

"That will come across as artificial."

"Do you think our audience will mind? They'll be licking ice cream, snogging, or having a nap until the film they bought a ticket to actually see starts."

He knew that Rowena would hear what he said next, so he declared in a clear voice. "It's our duty to make the film as interesting and as informative as possible. After all, these productions are part of the war effort."

"Yes, they are," Meg said, although she raised an eyebrow in surprise. "You're not the cynical young man I thought you were." Then she glanced at Rowena before murmuring so only he could hear. "Ah, the penny drops as your sap rises, my dear." In a louder voice she asked, "Jack. What do you suggest to make our little film as interesting and informative as possible?"

"Have our factory girl take a photograph of her boyfriend from her bag – he must be in a pilot's uniform – and put it next to the drill on the workbench. She can deliver the same lines, as near as damn it, to the love of her life, even though he's away fighting to save the free world from fascism."

"Good thinking, Jack." Meg nodded appreciatively. "That will provide an emotional hook."

"She drills holes for love as well as duty."

"All right, Jack, don't ladle the syrup too thickly. I just might gag."

He saw the director was joking; he laughed.

Meg turned to Rowena who examined her gorgeous, pouting lips in a mirror the makeup girl held for her.

"Rowena, dear. I want to get some shots of you operating the drill before we film you speaking your lines."

"Yes, Mrs Mercer." Rowena went to stand in front of the electric drill, fixed to a steel frame on the workbench. A box of C-Clips lay within reach. These were the metal blanks waiting to have a hole drilled into each end.

Jack knew that the C-Clip, supposedly ensuring that a machine gun would never jam, was pure invention for the story. During wartime, a film would never be shown to the public that featured details of manufacturing newly-developed components for weapons. After all, Nazi spies might be licking ice creams in the audience, too.

Meg asked the camera operator if he was ready. He nodded.

"Close up on the drill-bit," she said. "I want to see the point of the drill biting into the metal. Then pull out to the worker's face… Oh, Rowena. Please give me your best look of concentration. Focus completely on your work. Show the audience how vitally important it is that you drill the holes precisely, because you know that the lives of our fighting men depend on the accuracy of your work. Everyone ready?"

After a chorus of 'yesses' from the crew, she nodded at Rowena who switched on the drill. The shed walls fired back echoes of the high-speed electric motor as the bit turned faster and faster.

Rowena placed a C-Clip under the spinning drill-bit. Her eyes fixed on the c-shaped piece of metal. Jack imagined her actually thinking 'I will work to the best of my ability. I will make perfect C-Clips. They will help win the war. This is important. This is vital."

Then the blurring column of light that was the drill-bit, revolving at a thousand rpm, caught her hair. Those blonde strands wrapped around the spinning steel in a split second, dragging her face into the drill.

The electric drill's scream, ultimately, wasn't as loud as the shriek that left the actresses' throat. Blood spraying from her scalp turned out to be much redder than the lipstick on her mouth.

Jack raced back to the office building to telephone for an ambulance. The pain inside his stomach felt equal to a huge hand reaching inside of him to twist his intestines until they tightened to the point of snapping. On the stairs he met Frankie, the office boy.

Frankie smiled at him. Then spoke in a soft purr: "I'm going to be your own personal monster. I'm going to make you suffer. And suffer you shall before you die."

Jack punched Frankie in the face, knocking him flat against

25

the stairs.

After Jack had made the telephone call for the ambulance, he threw himself down onto his knees to go through the wastepaper basket, searching desperately for the slip of paper with the address: the one where he'd find two men who claimed to be Sherlock Holmes and Doctor Watson.

3. Behold: A Mystery of Singular Strangeness & Dread

Snowflakes streamed from the night sky, shrouding the black ash of destroyed houses with a pure white sheet. The bomber assault of the previous night had claimed over two hundred lives in Britain's capital. Men, women, children. Tonight there would be no bombing raids. Nazi planes were surely grounded by blizzards raging through occupied Europe. So: no air-raid sirens; no bombs; no death.

Jack Crofton trudged past the post office building in the heart of Fitzrovia. He wanted to write poetry about the enemy attacks that cascaded metal cylinders of high explosive from the sky. That need formed a dull ache in his stomach. Releasing pent-up emotion inside of him in torrents of verse would feel good. He'd feel relaxed again. But these days he never had the time. Working on film scripts filled his day. Nor were there spare moments in the evening: somehow he always ended up in a pub after work; the hours would melt away into a beery haze.

He walked through near darkness along Merchant Terrace, a canyon formed by tall buildings. Blackout regulations meant that no lights shone through windows. They'd all be screened by heavy curtains. Similarly, the streetlights were switched off, so they wouldn't act as a lure for enemy aircraft. If it wasn't for snow gleaming on the ground he'd probably be stumbling along in blackness equal to that found in the depths of a coalmine.

A moment later, he found the address he was looking for. He paused, thinking back to the dreadful events of the day. How Rowena's hair had been caught by the spinning drill-bit, dragging her head into that whirling bolt of steel, ripping out blonde locks, splitting her scalp, anointing the studio with her blood. The spray jetting from the wound had been crimson – a mist of red that seemed to fill the building. He'd felt it settle on his lips. He tasted the beautiful woman's blood with his tongue.

An ambulance had taken Rowena to hospital. The nurses hadn't allowed Jack to visit Rowena yet, as she'd be sent to sleep on a gentle stream of morphine; however, they reassured Jack that his girlfriend would recover fully. Jack decided to buy her flowers – they'd have to be paper flowers: no fresh blooms would be for sale in wartime London in winter. Tomorrow, he'd also have to explain to Mr Jensen why he had hit the office boy, Frankie. Of course, he couldn't give the real reason: that Frankie had issued a strange threat to make Jack suffer before he died. Jack already had a troubling reputation for being a heavy drinker – now he couldn't help but picture the prospect of himself standing in front of Mr Jenner as the man tore up the new contract bearing Jack's name. "We won't need this anymore, Crofton. Now, please collect your personal possessions from your desk and leave the building…"

Not eager to descend the steps to the basement flat, but almost as if a cold hand had reached out of the earth to press him between the shoulder blades, he found himself going down to a door that had precious little paint and was barely secured in place by a rotting frame – he tapped the knocker.

London had fallen under a deathly spell of silence because of the heavy snowfall, so he could make out shuffling sounds from the other side of the door, followed by the clunk of a bolt being drawn back. The door opened a few inches. A round face hung there, almost as if not attached to a body.

"Mr Crofton. You are a punctual man. Dead on seven."

Jack nodded by way of hello. "You're still interested in taking on my..." Saying the next word seemed odd, as if he consented to leaving the real world behind. "...case?"

"That depends..."

Jack raised a bottle to eye-level in the gloom. "As agreed."

"Of course, of course." The man who claimed he was Doctor Watson smiled. "Come in, come in."

Jack entered the basement flat. The floors were stone. The air inside seemed colder than outside. The walls consisted of whitewashed brickwork. They were badly in need of a fresh coat, yet the place smelt pleasantly of soap. When Jack made small talk about the snow he noticed puffs of white jetted from his mouth. If the rest of the flat was as cold then the two men must be enduring lives of freezing poverty.

Watson led Jack along the corridor to a doorway at the far end. Watson lightly tapped on the door.

"Come." The voice from the other side rang with authority.

Watson opened the door, then invited Jack to enter first. Jack found a small room lit by a table lamp. Coal smouldered in the grate. Along one wall, a single bed. Thick purple curtains covered the window. Three armchairs that didn't match each other were arranged in front of the fire to make the most of its dull warmth. Jack noted that despite the old furniture standing on worn out carpet the room was clean. Almost clinically so.

The gaunt man, Sherlock Holmes, or so he claimed, wore a black dressing gown embroidered with gold thread. The garment could easily have dated back to the last century. The fabric at the elbows consisted of stringy holes. He stood next to the fire, smoking a pipe.

Watson spoke quickly. "He brought whisky."

"Then three glasses, if you please, Watson."

As Watson selected three tumblers from a shelf, bearing oddments of glassware, Holmes said, "Mr Crofton, do take a seat.

29

The leather chair is the most comfortable."

Jack thanked him as he sat down. The single bed almost touched the arm of the chair. A checked blanket had been pulled over the mattress, covering a pillow.

Watson handed Jack a tumbler with a tiny drop of whisky in the bottom. The glass he offered to Holmes, and the glass he kept for himself, had been filled to the top.

Jack said, "Last night, in the pub, you said you could help me."

Holmes settled himself into the chair opposite him. "I'm sure I can." He took a mouthful of whisky, swallowing the amber sprit with obvious pleasure. "Although first I must interview you in detail."

"Oh?"

Watson added, "We need to have the measure of our client."

"And know his life in intimate detail," Holmes added. "After all, the clue to solving the mystery might lie closer to home than you think."

"If you think that will help." Jack felt more doubtful about this visit. Surely, these two oddballs couldn't help him.

"Proceed." Holmes closed his eyes. "Tell me your life story."

Despite powerful misgivings he did as Holmes asked. "My name is John Bernard Crofton, but I've always been called Jack. I'm thirty-three years of age. I was born in Yorkshire. My father's a coal miner. Our family didn't have much money. Neck of mutton stew on Sunday, leftovers on Monday, leftovers of the leftovers on Tuesday. I grew up with a love of reading. By the age of fourteen I'd already decided to become a poet. My mother encouraged me. My father discouraged me; quietly, yet persistently."

"Your mother encouraged you?"

"Yes, she believed sons didn't have to follow in their father's footsteps. You see, I come from a town full of generations of coal miners and generations of millworkers. My father wanted me to become a miner, too.

"Then your mother has quite progressive attitudes?"

"Her views were probably formed by seeing what happened

30

to her brother. He was wounded in the trenches in World War 1. After the war ended, he didn't go back to his old job at the pit. He could play the violin so he joined a string quartet that performed at tea dances in hotels in Eastbourne. My mother said that life as a musician was the making of her brother."

"Proceed."

Watson nodded. "Very informative. Most useful."

Both men continued to drink as Jack talked. Jack began to suspect that they'd only be interested in what he had to say while the Scotch lasted. Already, he found himself wanting to say a curt, "Good night. It's time I was going," then simply walking out, leaving them to finish the alcohol they so clearly craved. Then again... The events of yesterday: the downright frightening warnings that his own 'personal monster' intended to make him suffer before he died, prevented him from leaving. He had to get to the bottom of this. After all, the police wouldn't take him seriously if he went to them with a complaint that strangers had made bizarre threats. What's more, Rowena had been hurt today – and Frankie had repeated the warning; therefore, he could not dismiss what happened yesterday as a hallucination brought on by too much beer.

So, despite his unease at sitting in a room with two men, who professed to be Sherlock Holmes and Dr Watson, he told them about his life. Leaving school at fifteen. Writing poems in his bedroom at home. Fiery arguments with his father. Selling a poem to *The Times*. His mother's pride at seeing her son's name in the newspaper above a sonnet he'd composed about pit yard nightingales. This contrasted with his father's misery after being mocked by workmates in the miner's cage that took them deep underground: "Your lad away with the fairies, then, Charlie?" "Does Jack prance about in velvet britches, waving a daffodil in the air?"

Payment for the sonnet arrived from *The Times*: equivalent to his father's wage for an entire week, hacking coal in a three-foot-high tunnel, amid choking dust and blackness.

"On my twenty-eighth birthday, I moved to London. That was the week after Britain declared war on Germany. I earned a pittance washing dishes in hotels, sleeping anywhere I could, and writing poetry in pubs. In 1940 JM Dent published my first collection of poetry. There were good reviews. The book sold out all three hundred copies of its print-run. If it wasn't for shortages of paper due to the war the publisher would have reprinted the book. The following year I happened to be at a party where I met a film director. He told me that the government's Ministry of Information would offer the production company he worked for a lucrative contract if they could deliver ten scripts for ministry approval by the end of the week. These were for the type of films that are supposed to boost public morale. The director confided in me that they wouldn't have time to write the required number of scripts – they were two short. I offered to have a go. He said 'Yes, by all means do so – although we can't pay you if we don't get the contract'. Well, I wrote two scripts in four days. The director I'd met then had enough material to submit to the ministry. The film company were awarded the contract, which was worth a fortune to them."

Doctor Watson nodded with admiration. "Therefore, your hard work saved the day."

Holmes added, "I trust you were adequately rewarded?"

"They took me on the payroll as a scriptwriter. For the first time I earned enough to rent my own home. I've a very nice attic flat in Ladbroke Grove." He smiled. "I call it my tree house. The branches of a tree outside almost touch the windows. I'm very happy there."

"Capital," murmured Watson. "Absolutely capital"

"My employer allows me writing days – that's when I can work on scripts at home."

As levels of the spirit in the bottle dropped, so the two men sank deeper into their chairs, their bodies becoming limp; the alcohol generously stroking their worldly cares away.

"Tell us…" Holmes closed his eyes. "Tell us what happened

to you yesterday."

"There's nothing more than I can add to what I told you in the pub last night. A wounded soldier stopped me in an alleyway. After asking why I wasn't in uniform, he said 'I'm going to be your own personal monster. I'm going to make you suffer. And suffer you shall before you die'. Those were his exact words."

Holmes opened his eyes. They were drowsy, unfocussed. "Do you have any enemies?"

"My father."

Watson shook his head. "A sad state of affairs." He refilled the glasses, apart from Jack's. In fact, Jack realised he'd not touched that small drop of whisky that had been poured into his glass just after arriving here. Perhaps instinct dictated he should remain sober for once.

Holmes sipped the spirit. "So – no arch enemies." He gave a melancholy smile. "After all, I think we should disregard any notion your father might want you dead."

"I don't suppose he would murder me in the literal sense."

"Doctor Watson and I will conduct enquiries tomorrow... see if we can uncover clues pertinent to your case."

Watson spoke firmly, "Although payment must be agreed. The world's greatest detective, Mr Sherlock Holmes, does not apply his formidable intellect for free."

Jack couldn't stop himself. The two men, posing as Holmes and Watson, suddenly appeared so absurd he longed to yell at them. Although he managed to restrain from shouting, he forcibly asked, "Tell me this, you say you are Sherlock Holmes and Doctor Watson. How can you be serious about that? Holmes and Watson are fictional characters. They don't exist."

Watson blinked in surprise. "We are here before you."

"Flesh and blood," added Holmes, his gaunt face turning even more skull-like in the dim light of the table lamp.

"Conan Doyle invented the characters. They appear in stories."

Holmes fixed Jack with a piercing glare. "What are you really saying, Mr Crofton? That you don't require our help?"

"Just look at this from my point of view. Here I am, with two men who tell me they are characters from fictional stories. This isn't even Baker Street. You live in…" He barked the word: *"Poverty!"*

Doctor Watson's already scarlet face burned with anger. "Are you accusing us of insanity?"

"After all." Holmes spoke smoothly. "You, yourself, insisted you sat in a cinema where you saw Doctor Goebbels speak to you from a newsreel film."

"That happened. That really did." Jack sensed his childhood stammer trying to lay hold of his tongue again after all these years. "I-I'm telling the truth."

"Watson," said Holmes, "please give Mr Crofton another tot."

Watson poured a drop of Scotch into Jack's glass.

Sherlock Holmes sat up straight, his hands clasped together on his lap. He spoke in kind, gentle tones: "Look… Jack…. Believing we are Holmes and Watson must be difficult. However, the truth is we were quite a team once – solving crimes, helping the police, bringing criminals to justice. That was before we encountered a lean spell financially; something we could only resolve by selling our case notes to Sir Arthur Conan Doyle."

"Cases that the fellow clumsily rendered into fiction," Watson pointed out. "Without the good grace to change our names so we would remain anonymous. Our clients, always publicity conscious at the best of times, simply deserted us."

"I should be going," Jack said, feeling awkward in the men's presence. "Sorry to have troubled you."

Holmes looked him in the eye. "We can help. If you let us."

"I am frightened by what has happened, that's true. I'm especially frightened for the people I care about, because I think this monster is going to hurt my friends in order to make me suffer."

"There, it's settled, then." Watson's blue eyes twinkled. "For a bottle of whisky a day we will find this wretched monster that plagues you."

Holmes' gaunt face managed something close to a tender smile. "If our names trouble you, simply imagine that we've adopted the guise of Holmes and Watson to cloak our true identities, and that we are really employed by the military's Secret Service. However, seeing as our good friend, namely yourself, needs our help, we have decided to investigate a mystery of such an extraordinary nature that the police would not know where to begin."

"Hear, hear." Watson chuckled. "A capital solution. After all, ever since the war began we find ourselves – all of us! – living in a topsy-turvy world."

Holmes drained his glass. "A world where a frustrated artist from Austria becomes ruler of half of Europe. Ah... come, Watson. We'll retire to the kitchen for a while – allow our friend time to consider our proposal."

"A bottle of whisky a day." Watson stressed each word carefully. He then eyed Jack's glass. "Drink your drink, old boy. Don't let the good stuff dry out before you've had chance to have a taste."

They left Jack alone in the room with its bed and little coal fire. Coal that his father might have dug from the ground. Jack put his glass on the mantelpiece without so much as a sip. After that, he glanced around the room, realising he might find evidence of who the two men really were. In the back of his mind, he still suspected that they were either delusional, or conmen who planned to trick Jack out of a pint of booze a day in return for nothing in particular. He found two envelopes behind a clock on the mantelpiece: one addressed to 'the occupier', another for 'Miss Bridewell'. The address was the same as this one. The postmark told him the letter had been posted twelve years ago. Perhaps it had arrived long after the previous tenant Miss Bridewell had left. For some reason the two men had never thought to throw the letter away or hand it in at a post office. A drawer in the table revealed pieces of string, pencils, buttons and an empty gin bottle. He'd hoped to find more correspondence or even a rent book that would reveal the true names of the tenants of these dismal rooms.

He turned his attention to a coal scuttle. There were pieces of coal in the bottom along with a few sheets of paper. One piece was covered with handwriting. In fact, the same writing as the slip of paper on which Watson had written the address last night in the pub. Jack pulled out the paper.

This is what he read:-

THE CASE OF THE FEARFUL WRITER
By Doctor John Watson

Holmes and I had not long taken our seats in a little tavern not far from Fleet Street when a wild-eyed gentleman approached us.

"What do you make of him?" asked Holmes.

"Agitated, I'd say," I replied. "Probably caught up in the blitz and run ragged by fright."

The stranger gasped, "My name is Jack Crofton. I am pursued by monsters. Gentlemen, I need your help."

Footsteps from the other side of the door reached Jack. He quickly thrust the paper into his jacket pocket.

The door opened, Holmes and Watson stepped through.

Holmes stood there, hands thrust deep into his dressing gown pockets. "Sir? Have you reached a decision?"

The words, 'I don't need your help, after all' almost left Jack's lips. However, he pictured Rowena being carried to the ambulance on the stretcher. He realised that, apart from his mother, he cared about Rowena most in the world. Jack believed that some evil force had entered his life to bedevil him by hurting the people he knew.

"Yes," Jack declared with utter conviction. "I want you to help me. But God knows how you will, because I really do believe that I've been marked for death."

4. Approaching Monsters Cast Their Shadows Before Them

He stepped out from the gloomy, subterranean flat, his feet leaving prints in freshly fallen snow. The streets of Fitzrovia were empty. Wartime blackout regulations that stipulated people must not show any light from their windows meant that darkness turned the buildings into gigantic tombstone shapes that were absolutely black. The only sound: the scrunch of his feet in snow. Scents of charred wood from houses, destroyed by bombs in recent weeks, still ghosted through the air to reach his nostrils. Sometimes the aroma of burnt meat. Perhaps an overcooked supper, or an overlooked charred corpse beneath rubble. Here and there, he made out gaps in rows of shops and houses where constant air raids had obliterated buildings.

Jack Crofton paused as searchlights, way off to the north, suddenly blazed into life. Earlier, the radio news had reassured listeners that there would be no enemy attacks on Britain tonight due to atrocious weather on the Continent, which was now, virtually in its entirety, controlled by Hitler's armies. Certainly, he hadn't heard the warning sirens. All was silent. Perhaps the operators of the searchlights were simply taking part in a training exercise. Searing columns of light shone directly up into the sky to strike the underside of snow-bearing clouds, forming radiant disks that slowly skated back and forth.

As Jack watched, the disks began to form into what resembled human faces that stared down at him with hate-filled eyes. He recognized the wounded soldier that had attacked him last night. The face of the prominent Nazi Joseph Goebbels leered – rat-eyed, black-toothed. Beside that floated the features of Frankie, the office boy.

Jack stared up at the faces, seemingly projected onto the clouds. They grew larger. He realised they were descending – swooping down at him. Slowly, he began moving backwards, his heart beating faster. Not for the first time the words 'I'm going mad' ran through his head with a terrifying power. Insanity would explain everything. A descent into paranoia, hallucination. A complete separation from reality. He saw himself straitjacketed in a hospital bed, grimacing, shouting, convulsing, laughing.

Shadows moved ominously along the street. The shadows of marching men, cast by the glow of searchlights reflected back from the clouds. A gentle breeze touched him. A monster had exhaled its cold breath onto his face, or so it seemed to him. He shivered so violently his teeth snapped together, painfully nipping his tongue.

Then the soldiers came – twenty or more. They wore the pale brown uniforms of the Home Guard, their faces twisted with hate. Each man carried a rifle with a bayonet fixed to the barrel, the blade glinting.

The men marched toward him with determined expressions. He saw murder in their eyes.

A woman, with full red lips and glittering eyes, stepped out of the shadows nearby. "So it is," she purred. "You suffered before you died. Poor Rowena. Poor you."

Jack stumbled away from the stranger. His feet slithered awkwardly on the snow, causing him to lose his footing. He fell flat onto his back. Even though he'd fallen, he kept his gaze locked onto the faces of the Home Guard solders. Their eyes blazed with fury as they closed in on their victim, raising their rifles, preparing to stab the foot-long blades of their bayonets into his body.

A figure loomed above him, reached down and grabbed his arms. The elderly man had a ferocious strength. He dragged Jack to his feet as the soldiers closed in.

Jack realised he looked into the face of Sherlock Holmes. Nose-to-nose. They were just inches away from each other.

The soldiers were getting ever closer. As they marched, they tensed their bodies, ready to slaughter him, eager to see pure white snow turn red.

Holmes shouted, "No, Jack! I will not let you kill yourself!"

"I'm not responsible. This is nothing to do with me!"

"Run, man! Run!"

The red-lipped woman called after them: "Jack Crofton wanted this. He brought it on himself."

Holmes pointed to an alleyway as he ran. "In there."

Jack followed.

As if a spell had been broken, the soldiers shouldered their rifles as if they were on parade. They marched past the alleyway without even glancing in Jack's direction. Moments later, they were gone.

Holmes tried to catch his breath. "I'm afraid the lady is telling the truth."

Jack's heart pounded. "You knew this would happen – so you followed me. You knew the monster would try and kill me tonight."

Holmes nodded – his face as serious as that of a doctor with bad news for a patient. "I did. You see, I discovered the identity of the monster. And now you have, too."

5. Midnight, and the Monster in the Mirror is...

In the distance, a church clock struck midnight. Twelve chimes shimmered faintly through the windows into the hospital ward where twelve empty beds stood in rows against white, sterile walls. The thirteenth bed had an occupant. Pale faced, bandaged head, bruised eyelids closed.

Jack Crofton sat in a chair beside the bed. Sherlock Holmes occupied a second chair next to Jack's.

After a long silence Holmes murmured, "Is this your sweetheart?"

"Sweetheart?" Jack gave a grim smile. "I've never heard anyone actually called that before."

"Girlfriend?"

"I've known Rowena for a while. We work for the same film studio. She acts. She's very talented. In fact, far better than the parts I write for her."

"So you are very fond of Rowena?"

"Yes." Jack gazed at the sleeping woman, the morphine making her respiration so slow that that at times he feared she'd stopped breathing altogether. "And now, Mr Holmes, you tell me that my own personal monster is me. That somehow, due to my own perverse, self-destructive nature, I've brought this entity into existence – a demon that will punish me by hurting people I care about."

"Do you accept my theory?"

"Five years ago, we could not have believed that British cities would be systematically destroyed by Nazi aircraft. Now it's an everyday reality. Therefore, why shouldn't I believe that a monster, which once lived inside my mind, has manifested itself in the outside world? I've read about monstrosities of the psyche in Freud's work, so…" He shrugged. "Yes, recent events force me to believe what you've told me."

"Then my task is to save you from yourself… and others from you." Holmes glanced at Rowena's pale-as-death face. "Doctors say she will recover?"

"There will be scarring. Thankfully, though, because the drill only tore her scalp, her hair will grow over any signs of disfigurement."

"You love her?"

"Yes."

"Does the lady love you?"

Jack shook his head. "A casual boyfriend, that's how she sees me. She also knows I drink too much. What's more, I will go back to being a poverty-riddled poet when the studio fires me – which they will, sooner or later."

A flurry of voices made Holmes glance back. A pair of men in white coats wheeled a patient along the corridor on the other side of the open door. The voices faded quickly.

Holmes said, "A nurse told me that the hospital was evacuated this morning because an unexploded bomb was found nearby. That's the reason why Rowena has an entire ward to herself, which explains them permitting us to sit with her outside visiting time."

"I take it the unexploded bomb has been dealt with?"

He nodded. "As I shall deal with the unexploded bomb inside your head."

"I thought you were a detective, Mr Holmes. You sound more like a psychiatrist."

"Detective work involves a fair degree of psychology, too. After all, without a human mind deciding to commit a crime, there can be no crime to solve. *Mens Rea* and *Actus Reus*: legal terms for the guilty mind coupled to the guilty act."

"Did you and Doctor Watson solve many crimes?"

"Oh, yes, Jack. Hundreds, especially in the early years."

"And did Doctor Watson really write the cases down as stories?"

"He attempted to do so – regrettably, magazine editors never considered them penned dramatically enough to be suitable for publication. They claimed they were rather ponderous in style. That's why he agreed to hand his case notes over to Sir Arthur Conan Doyle, who succeeded in reworking them into something altogether melodramatic. The public found his dramatizations agreeable entertainment."

Jack pulled a sheet of paper from his pocket. "I found this in your coal scuttle."

Holmes smiled. "And you decided to steal it?"

"It's the beginning of a story written by Doctor Watson. He has me as a character coming to you for help."

"Don't fear embarrassment, Jack. The story will never be published. My friend, Watson, is feeling his years. His mind is no longer the sharp blade of old. He sits at his little desk in his room and scribbles for an hour or so, then gives up." He shrugged. "Watson is a faded portrait of his former self. The old chap is declining and I fear that within a few months I shall be alone. Knowing that makes me value him even more. The hours I spend in his company become more and more precious. If only I could have understood the real value of what's important in life when I was younger." He gave a sad smile. "But that's always the way – isn't that so? We don't appreciate what's precious until we lose it… or are on the threshold of that precious gift being taken from us. You must have thought likewise when you witnessed Rowena's

42

accident." He handed the sheet back to Jack. "Keep my friend's words as a souvenir of your visit."

They were silent for a while, watching the sleeping Rowena.

Eventually, Jack said. "When we first came into the ward I happened to glance in the mirror on the wall over there."

"Oh, yes?"

"You claim I am the monster that is tormenting me. Yet, I don't see anything different in my eyes."

"You fear you are insane."

"Well, aren't I?"

"No."

"You're hopeful that you can somehow get rid of the monster?"

"I am certain there is a way to prevent the evil inside of you attacking your good self and others."

"How will you do that?"

Holmes steepled his fingers together beneath his chin. "We must find a way of speaking to that inner beast of yours – then we shall discover why he has declared war on you."

6. Until Tonight

Aromas of frying bacon made Jack's mouth water. His stomach rumbled. He realised he hadn't eaten since Rowena's accident yesterday. At least he didn't suffer the headache of his customary morning hangover. Last night, when he'd visited Holmes and Watson in their basement flat, he hadn't drunk any alcohol.

Outside, in the corridor, office staff trooped toward the canteen for their mid-morning bacon sandwich. Across the yard in the studio, another actress had taken Rowena's place at the drill, pretending to make war-winning C-Clips for machine guns. Jensen, the studio boss, had insisted that shooting must be completed today in readiness for editing later in the week. He had even made a speech to his staff: "Our patriotic duty is to complete the film. It's what Rowena would have wanted. We are part of the war effort, too."

Jack longed to tell Jensen that Rowena was still alive, and the 'it's what she would have wanted' phrase was applied to women who were dead. But the shock of yesterday's gruesome incident had come back so forcefully when he saw a strand of hair, coated in dried blood, on the studio floor that he couldn't even whisper, let alone berate the odious man.

Frankie poked his head through the door. His right cheek

bore a graze that Jack had inflicted with his knuckles. "Bacon sandwiches going fast, old man. Chop, chop."

"Frankie...I'm sorry I hit you yesterday. I thought you were..."

Frankie had already gone. Jack felt a sudden overwhelming emotional warmth for the kid. Those were the first words that Frankie had spoken to him since Jack had punched him. Jack interpreted the prompt to go grab a sandwich as Frankie saying, 'I understand. You were upset about what happened to Rowena. I know you didn't really mean to hurt me.'

Jack rose from his chair just as the telephone rang on his desk.

He pressed the cold earpiece to his ear. "Hullo."

"Come to 26 Beech Crescent tonight. Six sharp."

"Is that you, Mr. Holmes?"

"You sound surprised."

"How did you know where I worked?"

"I am Sherlock Holmes. If I couldn't locate your telephone number, then that would make me a decidedly incompetent detective."

Jack asked, "Are we going to meet someone?"

"Yes, a gentleman has invented an electrical device that might help you. After all, you recall that last night in the hospital I explained that I needed to speak to your 'inner-beast' – that demon inside of you, which is bringing misfortune to yourself and your friends."

"What kind of device? And who is it, exactly, I'll be seeing?"

Holmes didn't answer Jack's questions. Instead, he crisply stated: "Six o' clock. 26 Beech Crescent. The street is close to Alexander Palace. We'll rendezvous there. Bring the whisky, and as much chocolate as you can acquire."

"Chocolate?"

"Chocolate, due to rationing is extremely scarce. Our inventor friend likes chocolate; he will accept that as payment."

"I understand." The world during wartime was indeed a topsy-turvy place. Jack knew full well that items such as chocolate, silk stockings, whiskey, canned peaches, and the like, were in short supply leading to them having a greater value than their mere cash price. "I'll be there, Mr Holmes."

"Bring a friend. A man as trustworthy as he is strong."

"Strong? Why the need for physical strength?"

"He might have to restrain you. Or knock you out, if the experiment is a failure." Holmes paused for a moment, no doubt considering an even more disturbing outcome. "Or, indeed, if the experiment is a success."

"What you're saying does worry me a lot."

"Oh, indeed. What we undertake tonight will be dangerous, extremely dangerous."

"Will Doctor Watson be there?"

"Alas, no. He's not in the best of health today."

"I'm sorry to hear that."

Holmes' voice evoked nothing less than sadness. "And I am sorry to see him so."

"I'll bring a friend."

"Until tonight, Jack. Until tonight."

7. Sounds of Terror. Visions of Death

Jack Crofton sat in the living room of 26 Beech Crescent. Even though night had fallen by the time he'd arrived at the house, he had made out the gigantic structure of Alexander Palace, standing on its hill, overlooking the flat, low-lying expanse of London – a mass of streets, buildings, public squares and parks. The weather had turned a little milder, thawing the snow, until all that remained were streaks of grey mush at the sides of the roads.

The room smelt strongly of boiled pears, perhaps more evidence of the homeowner's sweet tooth. After all, the man's eyes had gleamed behind the thick lenses of his glasses as he hurried away to the kitchen, carrying the chocolate that Jack had manged to procure with his build-up of unused sweet ration coupons. When the war began, the government, realising that many products would soon be in short supply, due, in the main, to enemy submarines sinking cargo ships bound for Britain, had issued ration books to every household. After all, Britain depended on food imports to feed itself. This meant that certain items, including meat, eggs, sugar, butter, as well as clothes, and petrol for cars, could only be purchased when the customer, in addition to paying

47

the cash price for the goods, also handed over a coupon torn from their ration book. The government hoped this system of rationing would mean that food would be distributed fairly; therefore, the population would not starve if the war was a long one. Even so, shortages were widespread. People were going hungry. Here in 1944, criminals now preferred to steal a truck full of butter rather than jewels.

The chocolate-eater, aged forty or thereabouts, was a thin, worried-looking man in a green sweater and baggy trousers. Sherlock Holmes had introduced him as Bernard. Jack didn't know if Bernard was the man's first name or surname; not that he had time to ponder the matter, because Bernard didn't even utter one word of welcome. He'd merely pointed at a straight-backed chair in the living room and said, "Sit there."

Jack, as directed by Holmes, had brought his sculptor friend with him, Bill Tulley. Bill, a powerful man of thirty-four, stared at blocks of electrical equipment that surrounded Jack as he sat on the chair. Holmes and Bill had perched themselves on a bench that stood against one wall.

Bill pointed at the metal boxes, which were connected to each other with thick rubber- coated cables. "What does all that stuff do?"

"And do I have to sit so close to all these machines?" Jack added, feeling oppressed by the proximity of the coffin-sized objects that housed potentially dangerous high-voltages.

Holmes held up a hand. "I'm sure it's all essential for the experiment."

Bernard swiftly checked dials on the instruments. "A cathode ray tube will show a visual representation of electromagnetic activity inside the subject's brain." He switched off the main overhead light before switching on a small desk lamp that contained an orange bulb. Faces were transformed to the colour of rust in that dull light. "The lab must be gloomy in order for us to see the screen in detail. I'm going to activate the equipment now; the valves require a few moments to warm up."

48

Bernard continued making darting rushes around the room, flicking switches, checking cables, examining dials, then switching on the television. Its nine inch screen gave off a dim, silvery glow.

"How does this machine see into my head?" asked Jack.

Bernard snorted. "If you had six months to sit there while I explained, I doubt if you'd still understand."

Bill frowned. "Will Jack be in danger?"

"If I placed a cup of water on the chair, and turned the device up to its maximum output it would boil the water." Bernard puffed out his chest, his voice now boastful. "One day, electromagnetic waves will roast an entire chicken."

Holmes spoke soothingly, "I'm sure this particular experiment will not require such levels of power."

"No." Bernard sounded almost regretful. "No, it'll be quite safe."

Jack said, "To say it's wartime, you've acquired an awful lot of equipment." His eyes narrowed as he read words stencilled on a Bakelite box that sprouted cables. "Some of which say 'Army property' on the side."

Bernard hissed through clenched teeth. "Last week, I walked out of the research centre. My ideas are too big for those government idiots. They moan about fuel shortages. When I told them to convert cars to run on radio waves they just sneered. All they need do is replace petrol engines with electric motors, then erect high-power wireless transmitters in a uniform grid pattern across town – they wouldn't need their absurd fossil fuels then. What's more, they could cover factory roofs in selenium. Sunlight falling on the selenium generates enough electrical power to –"

Holmes interrupted, "Ahem. My good, sir." He leaned forward, fixing his sharp eyes on the boxes that now hummed gently, while emitting a yellow glow from air vents. "Indulge us. Explain succinctly how the machine works."

Bernard pointed at foot-long silvery metal rods that extended outward from a central core. They resembled the spokes of a bicycle wheel placed in a vertical position close to Jack's right ear.

"That, gentlemen, is the broadcast aerial. It transmits radio waves through the subject's skull. They pass through the brain and are moulded by the brain's natural electromagnetic pulses – laymen call these pulses 'thoughts'. When the radio waves emerge from the skull at the other side they are captured by the receiving aerial." Lightly, he touched copper rods that had been soldered into an H-shape, which also stood vertically six inches from Jack's left ear. "The waves then run through cables to something akin to radio valves that convert the stream of electrons into sound and vision, which are then displayed on that television screen." An expression of triumph lit up his face. "This is the part of the operation that is pure genius. Those streams of electrons that have passed through the subject's brain then loop around through these devices and are then transmitted back into the brain – round and round they go."

Bill frowned, clearly not understanding the explanation. "Why? What's this scientific wizardry for?"

Bernard's expression turned to one of annoyance. "I've just told you."

Holmes spoke in gentle tones. "What my friend here is driving at, is what do you hope the experiment will achieve?"

"Why, what you requested, Mr Holmes." Bernard patted a box set with dials, switches and meters. "This... My Cerebral Electromagnetic Repeater, will establish a communication link with those hidden psychological components of the mind."

Jack said, "You mean, talk to my subconscious?"

Bernard sniffed with contempt. "A layman might use the word 'subconscious' in such a slipshod fashion. This machine communicates with the psychological engines buried deep within that portion of the brain which generate dreams, governs instincts, stimulates..." His eyes gleamed behind his glasses. "... stimulates nascent compulsions."

"Art," Jack said.

"Sex," Bill corrected.

Bernard's frustration grew as he tried to explain his invention. "Look. It's all very simple. This device records the subject's brainwave activity and reflects it back into his head as electromagnetic pulses. It's like meeting a foreigner who doesn't speak English, and you don't speak their language, so you repeat some of the words they speak, and hey-presto, the foreigner realises you are striving to a communicate with them."

Bill appeared even more bewildered. "So our subconscious speaks a different language? Like French or Greek?

Bernard grunted, trying to suppress his irritation. "Rather than explain what all this equipment does, I will show you. Gentlemen, you will be astounded!"

He flounced through the door into the next room. Jack wondered if he'd gone to switch on more equipment, or eat chocolate.

Bill turned to Holmes. "Are you Jack's doctor? He told me that there was going to be some kind of medical experiment here tonight."

"Has he explained who I am?"

Bill shook his head.

Holmes said, "Consider me Jack's friend. I am trying to help him solve a rather singular problem."

Bill shot Jack a glance that plainly asked: *What the hell's going on here?*

Jack hadn't told Bill about the threats he'd received in the last three days. He simply said, "I can't explain now, Bill. Trust me."

Bill nodded. "You'd help me, no questions asked. I'll do the same."

"Spoken like a loyal ally." Holmes smiled warmly. "And tonight we shall perhaps get to grips with Jack Crofton's enemy."

The glass valves inside the boxes shone brightly as they warmed to full power. The hum grew louder. Jack felt the fillings in his teeth begin to tingle. There was a distinct odour of electricity in the air, something he was familiar with from spending time in the film studio – that odour told him that high voltages flowed through the cables to animate this electrical equipment. His muscles tightened. He could almost picture electricity leaping from the metalwork next to his head and into his body to crackle along his nerves. There was a sensation of pressure on his forehead.

No... behind my forehead. A pressure inside my skull. Pains darted through his teeth. He ran his tongue across his fillings. They felt hot – his tongue tingled when he touched them.

"Electricity's going into my body." Jack clenched his fists as he sat on the chair. "I can feel it... "

Holmes spoke soothingly again, "Don't worry. Everything will be alright. We are close to defeating the evil inside of you. "

Bill remained silent; however, Jack saw him glance at Holmes in astonishment. Yet, clearly, Bill understood that this unusual state of affairs in the room was designed to help Jack so he didn't leave his seat or ask questions.

Meanwhile, Holmes continued speaking. His voice was gentle... slow... almost the relaxing tones of a hypnotist. "Jack. Don't say anything, just listen to me. Not only am I speaking to you, Jack Crofton, I am also speaking to another part of you inside your head. That part of your mind that has rebelled against you. Doctor Sigmund Freud tells us that we possess something called Eros. Eros is our love of life – Eros is the instinct to survive, to have children and continue the human race. He also identified another part of our mind which he named the Death Drive. In his native German that is known as *Todestrieb*. Picture that section of your mind being like a powerful, vicious dog. Normally, your civilized instincts will restrain the Death Drive, but like a vicious dog that has slipped its collar and run amok, biting people, so your Death Drive has broken free. No longer restrained by the good side of your nature, the Death Drive is harming the people you know and, ultimately, that part of your own mind will force you toward your own self-destruction."

Bernard flicked switches on a control panel. The hum became a loud buzz. Sharp pains darted through Jack's skull. When his lips began to itch like fury he tried to raise his hands to rub his mouth. However, he couldn't move his arms. All he could do was sit, staring at Holmes and Bill Tulley on the bench, and the gleaming face of Bernard, who now positively quivered with excitement.

"Almost there," shouted Bernard. "Keep watching the television screen!"

Jack couldn't move his head; yet he managed to roll his eyes to the right, where he saw silvery lights flicker on the television. Was it his imagination, or did those patches of silver and darkness form the shape of a long face with eyes made of hundreds of glittering points of light?

At that moment, the air-raid siren wailed in the distance.

Bill rose to his feet. "We should go to the shelters."

"Forget the raid." Bernard's voice shook with nothing less than exhilaration. "Those fluctuations of light on the screen echo the subject's waves of thought. I am close to a historic breakthrough!"

A powerful hiss leapt from a loud speaker fixed to the wall.

Bernard turned a dial. Jack's spine arched; his head tilted back; he panted as if he'd been running for his life.

Bernard stared at the screen in absolute fascination. "Mr Holmes. Speak to what's in the subject's head. Interrogate the creature."

The involuntary muscle spasms hurt Jack. He longed to escape from the house into the cold night air and breathe, just breathe. Yet he could not move his body as he wished. His teeth felt as if they were burning inside his mouth. He wanted to scream but all that came out were throaty, gasping sounds.

Holmes stood up, fixed Jack with those deep-set eyes and spoke in commanding tones. "You, who occupies Jack Crofton's head: I know what you are. I know that you are hell-bent on torturing the man by hurting others. Why?"

Jack feared his head would burst. The pressure inside of him grew and grew, hurting, burning, twisting, searing...

Holmes took a step closer. "Speak to me. Reveal why you are doing this."

Jack Crofton's mouth snapped shut, teeth clicking – those burning, hurting teeth that he'd gladly tear from his mouth, if only that would stop the pain.

"You are Todestrieb," Holmes thundered. "The Death Drive of the psyche. Ancient people also gave a name to you – and that name is Satan!"

Jack spoke. He didn't intend to... want to... The words could not be stopped. Awful words – dreadful life-hating words: "The war has set me free. Death sets everyone free. Because that's what the human race loves now. Thoughts of their death seduce them. They want to rid themselves of the awful burden they call Life. Life is hard, troublesome, painful. Life brings so much worry. Death is peace. Death is silence. Death is happiness." Jack heard the next words soar from his lips with all the glory and bright shining joy of souls released from misery – souls rising to the eternal joy of heaven. "DEATH IS LOVE."

Bill grabbed Holmes by the arm. "Stop this! Can't you see? Jack's dying... The machine's killing him."

"Unhand me! We are close to saving him!"

"Saving him? Look, blood's coming out of his nose. He can't breathe."

Bernard yelled. "Look at the screen... No, it can't be happening – it's impossible!"

Bill spun round to the man. "What is it? What's wrong?"

"Don't you see?"

Holmes disregarded the television set. Instead, he moved closer to Jack, staring into his eyes. "You in there, you must submit to Jack Crofton's will. The Death Drive is destructive. You must not urge human beings toward self-extinction."

Jack murmured softly, "There will always be war, poverty, sickness. Misery. Don't you see? To die cures everything. The dead don't suffer. The dead feel no pain..."

Bernard screamed, "Destroy the subject. Smash its skull." He snatched a hammer from the table and offered it to Holmes.

Bill thundered, "Are you insane?"

"Look at the screen," howled Bernard. "What do you see?"

Holmes flinched with surprise at what he saw blazing there in silver and deepest black. "Alexander Palace. As if we look down upon the building from a great height."

Jack managed to focus his eyes on the screen, too. This is what he saw there: the moon illuminating the landscape almost as bright as day. A clear image of the vast structure of Alexander Palace far below. He saw roads lined with houses nearby. A railway line ran along the foot of the hill. A steam locomotive moved along the track far below.

Holmes turned to Bernard. "What are we seeing? Explain."

Bernard's eyes were huge with fear. "The television has captured a transmission from a V1 – the Nazis have begun installing cameras on their vengeance weapons. The images are carried back to Berlin, via a short-wave transmitter, for Hitler's gratification. Hitler and his noxious henchmen will see what we're seeing now. A view of London from high in the air."

"Then, after that, what will they see?"

"They'll see the streets suddenly rush in closer and closer; houses getting bigger and bigger – faces in the windows, faces of children, faces of people who will be slaughtered when the flying bomb strikes and explodes and shreds human flesh."

Bernard appeared close to heart failure. He swayed there, clutching his chest, sweating, panting, grimacing – bulging eyes locked onto the screen.

Holmes gripped Bernard's arm. "How can killing Jack stop the V1 from striking the city?"

"Don't you see, Mr Holmes? The way his thoughts pulse across the screen at the same time the flying bomb changes direction. His mind steers the weapon now. He is in control. The only way to... to..." He gulped. "The only way to break his control over the flying bomb is to smash his skull with the hammer. If you destroy his brain the V1 will fall elsewhere."

Bill roared. "You can't kill Jack. I'll break your necks if I have to!"

Bernard sagged, dropping down into a chair, his gaze fixed to the television. "If you don't kill him, we will die. Look at the screen.

That's my house you can see. The V1 is approaching – the weapon will strike this building."

Even as the man spoke, Jack Crofton heard the distinctive burble of the V1's pulsejet motor. The sound grew louder. He watched the screen as rooftops slid by beneath the airborne weapon that carried a devastatingly lethal payload of more than a thousand pounds of high explosive. He controlled its flight, yet he didn't – not consciously – another force inside his head moved the rudder and elevator, steering the bomb toward Beech Crescent. When the right hand side of the screen pulsed brightly, the robot aircraft turned to the right. Likewise, when brightening on the left the machine then glided in that direction. The engine sound from outside became a roar, getting louder and louder. Windows rattled.

Onscreen, the distinctive curve of Beech Crescent, lined with houses, grew larger. The nose of the pilotless machine began to drop, the engine rose to a scream.

"Kill him!" Bernard shrieked, lunging forward, hammer raised.

"No!" Bill Tulley grabbed the man's wrist, preventing him from smashing the hammer down onto Jack's skull.

As the men struggled, Holmes began to speak softly yet firmly. "Fight the monster, Jack. Don't let it destroy you. Life is worth living." His thin fingers closed over Jack's shoulders. "Rowena… Picture Rowena. What would she tell you to do now?"

As Holmes uttered 'do now' the diving V1's murderous scream rose until the sound tore through the room with so much force that Bernard and Bill stopped fighting and clamped their hands over their ears.

Jack's eyes locked onto the television screen. He forced himself to imagine the top of the screen brightening. The image there showed the roof of 28 Beech Crescent expanding as the machine hurtled earthwards. From nearby houses, people fled for their lives. A woman carrying a baby reached a garden gate.

Too late. The V1's zone of destruction was five hundred yards in diameter. Both babe and women would be annihilated.

Holmes shouted, "Jack! Picture Rowena!"

The top of the screen brightened. The angle of the image changed. The V1's pointed nose must have been lifting. Chimney pots flashed by at either side. The aircraft skated through the air just twenty feet above roof tops. Alexander Palace flashed by to the right. In front lay open grassland bathed in moonlight. Beyond that, the dark mass of buildings that was London.

Jack willed the bright smear of silver light to move to the bottom of the screen. *Down… force the machine into a dive.* Trees filled the screen. Then an expanse of turf looming closer… closer. Abruptly, the televised scene crashed to black. Three seconds later a tremendous bang buffeted the house, shattering the living room windows. The blast-wave tore one of the curtains in two. That was all. The V1 had detonated on impact as its Nazi engineers intended; however, that murderous device had exploded in open parkland in front of Alexander Palace, distant enough not to destroy the houses or the people inside them.

Holmes tugged electrical plugs from wall sockets. Instantly, the once brightly glowing valves in the apparatus faded. Pains shooting through Jack's body vanished at the same moment.

Bernard sat hunched in a chair, softly weeping. Bill helped Jack to stand. Meanwhile, Holmes opened the living room door, indicating they should leave.

As Jack shuffled by, feeling wrung-out, exhausted, half dead, Holmes spoke to him. "You need to be with Rowena. She, the woman whom you love, is the only one who can thwart the monster inside of you."

8. A Weapon Sharper and More Certain than St. George's Lance

Jack Crofton moved in a daze, as if sleep walking. Sherlock Holmes and Bill Tulley guided him through the parklands in front of Alexander Palace. There, a huge crater, formed by the V1 plunging into the earth just minutes ago, still gave off steam. A pungent smell of burning prickled the inside of Jack's nose. Glittering fragments of the flying bomb littered the grass. Trees had been stripped of both bark and branches by the titanic blast. Jack knew that the pilotless craft, launched from those parts of Western Europe still under Nazi rule, were devastating weapons. He'd seen the aftermath of such a strike in Hounslow. The huge warhead exploded in what is termed 'the double hammer blow' – first, the blast-wave struck the nearest buildings, smashing inwards with such force that victims were thrown against inner walls with pulverising violence. After that, the blast rushed by creating a vacuum: the injured and dead occupants of the building were then sucked out through shattered windows into gardens and roads like dolls thrown by a bad-tempered child.

"You saved lives," Bill said as they walked past the crater, which smelt strongly of wet soil. "If the V1 had hit the street full of houses...." Completing the sentence was as unnecessary as forensically describing rubble strewn gardens containing mangled corpses.

Jack sucked in the cold night air, trying to clear the fog from his mind. "How could I make the machine crash where nobody would be hurt?"

Holmes said, "Due to something that the psychologist Carl Jung terms the Daemon – an inner personality that is wise and guides us. Daemon is at its most dynamic and inventive in times of crisis. We all carry that extraordinary component within our heads."

"Divine inspiration," Bill added.

Holmes shook his head. "Not divine. As natural as the fingers on your hands."

Jack's head began to clear. "You mentioned Rowena. How can she help me?"

"She did earlier, or rather the mental image you have of her."

"A guardian angel." This time Bill glared at Holmes, daring to contradict him.

"A guardian angel?" Holmes smiled. "Why not think of her thus? If that strengthens us in our battle against this wicked impulse that Freud called the Death Drive, then why not?"

Jack felt his strength returning, together with a growing determination to fight the monster nestled between his ears. "People in the office were saying that the hospital was going to discharge Rowena this afternoon. She's probably at home."

Holmes digested the information. "You know her address."

"Yes."

"Then guide us there, Jack. I suspect that the final battle between you and that personal monster of yours is getting close now. Very close."

9. A Slight Deviation

The route by Tube to Rowena's flat ran near enough to the Fitzrovia district of London for Sherlock Holmes to make a slight detour and check on how Watson was faring. Jack followed Holmes down the steps to the basement flat. He carried a brown paper bag that contained a bottle of whisky – the day's fee for Holmes' help. Bill said he'd wait in the street for them.

Holmes led the way into the living room. Jack saw that Watson lay on the bed, covered by the dressing gown that he'd seen Holmes wearing on his first visit here yesterday. The fire had gone out, leaving white ash in the grate. The air was deathly cold. Jack could see his breath.

Holmes asked gently, "How are you, old chap?"

Watson raised his eyelids slowly as if they were enormously heavy. "Can't complain, Holmes," he whispered. "Feeling much better. I'll light the fire... get you some supper."

"No, no, old fellow. Stay as you are. I'm going onto another destination tonight."

"Hah." Watson seemed very weak as he smiled. "The game is afoot."

"Assuredly so. Look. A tincture to warm yourself with." He nodded in the direction of the bottle that Jack pulled from the bag.

"Jack bought us a rather fine Scotch."

Watson raised his hand in greeting. "Thank you, sir. I'll get the glasses."

Holmes soothed the man, lightly patting his arm. "No. You stay there. I'll set you up with a tot before I go. You look as if you do with a nice warmer."

As Watson continued to lie under the dressing gown, with scarcely enough strength to keep his eyes open, Holmes fetched a glass, poured a generous measure, then knelt beside the bed so he could gently raise his friend's head, helping him drink.

"Thank you, Holmes." Watson smiled. "You know, I've been thinking about writing up what really happened that time in Cornwall... when the family believed that they were being hunted by a monstrous hound. Wouldn't the truth shake the ruling classes from top to bottom?"

Holmes spoke softly, "Why not? To the devil with Conan-Doyle. We shall use real names, and reveal what that animal truly was."

"Yes, I'm looking forward to that. The two of us working together on our first book." Watson shivered and Holmes carefully pulled a blanket over the man up as far as his chin.

Jack said, "I'll make up the fire before we go. It's like ice in here."

Holmes glanced back, his face appearing more gaunt than ever. "Completely out of coal, I'm afraid. My fault. I forgot to place an order."

Watson chuckled. "Holmes, you forget nothing. Absolutely nothing." He sighed as if feeling contented. "Don't you worry about the coal. I feel as warm as warm can be. That whisky has done the trick."

"I'll leave the glass here by the bed."

"Ah, would you help me drink a little more? I confess I'm so tired tonight I can hardly keep my eyes open."

"Of course, old chap. Of course." Holmes put his arm around his friend's shoulders and carefully lifted him so he could put the glass to his lips without spilling.

Jack found himself so moved by the poignant scene – two old friends nearing their limits of physical ability yet still striving to live normal lives. Suddenly he felt as if he was intruding on a private scene. "Mr Holmes, I'll wait outside. Good night, Doctor Watson. I hope you feel better soon."

He hurried back up the steps to where Bill leaned against the railings. A horse pulling a wagon clip-clopped along the street. The driver sat holding the reins with his head down, trying to use his upturned coat collar to protect himself from the icy night air.

Bill said, "It's been a rum do tonight. Demons in your head, scientific wizardry, almost been blown up by a V1 bomb. I was starting to think I'd died and gone to a funny kind of hell."

"I'm the poet. Leave lyrical metaphors to me."

He smiled. "Are we still going to Rowena's place?"

"In a minute. Mr Holmes is giving his friend some... medicine. He's not very well."

"Mr Holmes? Is that what they call him?" Despite the grimness of the night's events Bill laughed softly. "By any chance, his friend isn't called Doctor Watson, is he?"

"Would it be strange if he was?"

"Nothing's strange any more. I've just seen a dog run by with a man's hand in its mouth."

"I never know when you're joking."

"On Sunday night, I really did stand on part of a human face, you know? Eyeless... bristly beard."

"An exploding bomb can hurl bits of corpse anything up to half a mile away."

"My cousin took a photograph of a torso hanging from telephone lines."

Jack noticed the dog running back along the street with a dark object gripped between its teeth. Bill pretended to stare at his watch. Jack lifted his face to gaze up into the sky. They didn't speak until the dog with greedy, glittering eyes ran by with its tasty supper.

Then Jack patted Bill on the shoulder in a friendly way. "Thanks for coming with me tonight."

"My pleasure. You'll come to my funeral, won't you?"

"You'll live to be a hundred."

"I don't think I'll survive this war, Jack. I looked at my calendar today. December's page is missing. And we're approaching the end of November. Rather an ominous sign, don't you think?"

10. Beneath London Clay, Human Clay

Jack, Bill and Sherlock Holmes walked into Goodge Street Underground Station where they bought tickets before using a lift to descend to the platform. Already, dozens of people sat or lay on the platform, preferring to spend the night there than in their homes which were so vulnerable to Nazi bombs. The railway management had prohibited the use of these deep subterranean stations as bomb shelters but Londoners simply occupied the platforms anyway, rigging up makeshift beds for themselves and their children. In the end, station bosses just let them stay.

Underground trains still ran, so travellers had to thread their way through knots of people sitting on station platforms before they could board the carriages.

Jack and his two companions did this now as a train lumbered into the station. Jack smelt onion soup warming in a pan on a primus stove nearby. People sheltering here were striving for at least a partly normal life in these abnormal extremes of war.

The carriage was almost empty of passengers. Jack sat opposite Holmes and Bill as the train rumbled away along the track, which wormed its way through the earth almost one hundred and fifty feet beneath London's streets. When he glanced sideways through the window he saw his shadow projected by the carriage lights onto the side of the tunnel.

Jack's own personal monster, his Death Drive, as Holmes had termed that rogue element of his psyche, was as firmly attached to him as his shadow now cast upon the wall. However, that evil monster danced inside his head – dancing in love with death. His death. Jack struggled to understand what he'd been told. The Death Drive, as he understood the Freudian concept, resided inside everyone. Normally, that denizen of the human mind was restrained by stronger elements of the psyche. The instinct to continue living had the power to subdue the Death Drive. For some reason, in Jack the Death Drive had got the upper hand. In some subliminal way that monstrous part of him had taken control. The beast had erupted from its cage. Then, in a further grotesque twist, that loathsome thing appeared to have the ability to transmit its power into the heads of other people and control them, a concept he was struggling with. He recalled the wounded soldier who had attacked him. Could it be that all such incidents had happened only inside his own head? No, convenient though that explanation might be, it failed to explain how the rogue part of his mind had managed to take over the unmanned flying bomb, steering the machine toward the house near Alexander Palace. There was much about this he didn't understand, but he had to accept that the threat was genuine.

Jack wondered if the Death Drive had simply been gripped by a suicidal urge now. Perhaps all that mattered to the thing was the destruction of Jack Crofton. The single-minded lust for self-extinction.

The train pulled into another underground station. There were hundreds of people covered by blankets or sitting on cushions. They'd spend the night there until morning when the danger of attack would abate for a few hours. Nazi bombers generally struck during the hours of darkness, rarely by day when they'd be more vulnerable to anti-aircraft fire from the ground, as well as squadrons of vengeful British fighter planes.

The train rattled to a stop. Doors slid open to release passengers onto the platform.

And then, once again, that evil tenant within Jack Crofton's skull reached out to exert its malign influence. Because, one by one, the men, women and children on the platform stood up. They stared in through the carriage window at Jack. Their mouths began to move, all apparently uttering the same word; however, the hum of the train's electric motors was too loud to hear what they said.

Jack knew they all stared at him.

His heart beat faster. "It's happening again," he managed to say. "Somehow that thing inside of me is taking them over."

Bill turned to the window. "Just look at their faces. Look how angry they are."

Bill's words provided further proof that this was *not* all in Jack's head. He felt an overwhelming sense of gratitude to his friend just then.

Holmes held up his hand. "Keep calm. We'll be moving shortly."

Keep calm? Easier said than done. Jack stood up. His legs trembled. His heart pounded faster and faster. People surged toward the open carriage doors. Their hate-filled eyes locked onto Jack.

"They want me dead." He knew he was trapped here in the carriage. Where could he run?

"Sit down," Holmes commanded. "Breathe deeply."

"What? When those people want to kill me?"

At that moment the doors slid shut. With a lurch, and squeal of axles, the train accelerated back into the tunnel again. Thankfully, none of the platform people had the time to enter the carriage. Even now they would be returning to normal as that uncanny influence left them. Probably they didn't even know that, for a few seconds, they'd lost control of their bodies and minds. They'd pull blankets over themselves again, trying to sleep where sleep was impossible, as trains thundered out of the tunnel every five minutes.

Jack sat there with his fists clenched on his lap. Sweat trickled down his chest inside his clothes. A thoroughly unpleasant sensation. He licked his lips – they were dust dry.

He said: "That's going to keep happening, isn't it. Every man and woman I meet. They could become my murderer in the blink of an eye." He shuddered. "Even one of you might attack me."

He glanced from Holmes to Bill. They stared back at him, saying nothing.

Jack wished he could find some hideaway to crawl into. A place where he'd be alone. His eyes flicked from one man to the other. Danger blazed inside of him. A great pulsating red light that warned of Death strolling toward him with the smiling certainty that he couldn't out run its lethal touch.

"Why don't you say something?" he demanded. "Bill, why are you looking at me like that? Holmes. I'm depending on you to save me. Why are you just staring at me?"

"Jack..." Holmes took a deep breath. "We are just as we've always been. Aren't we, Bill?"

"Yes." Bill nodded. "But those people back there – they seemed to see something in Jack they despised. There was an overwhelming sense that they would have ripped him apart if they'd got their hands on him."

Jack heaved a sigh of relief. "Thank God, you're alright. I thought you'd turned, too."

Bill identified a problem. "But what if we aren't the same five minutes from now? What if that thing in Jack's head takes us over and makes us attack him?"

Tellingly, Holmes didn't reject the idea. "Then we must be vigilant."

"I can't watch you all the time," Jack protested. "I'm now expecting the second I turn my back on you I'll get my skull caved in."

"He's right," Bill said.

Holmes spoke with absolute conviction: "That's why we must hasten to Rowena's home."

Jack felt like a hunted man. "But how can Rowena help me?"

Holmes leaned forward to grip Jack's wrist while looking him in the eye, his expression grave. "Jack, my friend. Do you believe in the saying, 'Love conquers all'?"

"Is that your plan?" Jack, despite himself, felt the urge to laugh. "As protection goes that's as flimsy as a bomb shelter made out of toilet paper."

"You do love her?

"Yes."

"Then you must believe that love does triumph over adversity. Love sustains the human race. Believe that is so, because it's time we put your love for Rowena to the ultimate test."

The train roared through the tunnel, its engines rising in pitch until, to Jack's ears, it sounded as if they were screaming.

11. First Bombs, Falling

Jack left the station to find a bright moon shining down. A church clock struck ten. He and Bill Tulley and Sherlock Holmes walked swiftly in the direction of where Rowena lived on Clifton Avenue, a quiet street consisting of once grand houses now subdivided into small flats. They passed pubs that, although emitting no light, due to wartime blackout regulations, did release a flow of odours of tobacco and beer together with murmurs of conversation.

As they crossed Clifton Avenue the wail of air raid sirens began. A police constable blew his whistle to attract their attention.

The constable called across to them, "Sirs. There's a big raid coming – a hundred planes or more. You'll find a public bomb shelter down that way. Can't miss it, there'll be ARP men at the door."

He moved off toward a group of men and women spilling out of a pub. As he ran he blew his whistle before repeating the warning.

Holmes said, "We still need to find Rowena. I truly believe matters are coming to a head now. Jack is in the gravest danger."

Bill looked worried. "Jack. How far to Rowena's?"

"Almost there. The big house with iron railings."

Jack had seen the house a few times before when picking up

Rowena in the production company's van for a day's filming on location. He'd never been inside.

The siren continued its nerve-jangling howl, alerting London that waves of enemy planes were on their way. Its citizens would now be taking cover before high explosive weaponry began to obliterate houses and commercial premises alike. Holmes, despite his advanced years, moved quickly; he didn't even seem breathless. Jack panted hard, his breath showing as white plumes in the moonlight. Normally, Bill Tulley could be relied on for healthy portions of gallows' humour. Tonight, however, his serious expression tugged at Jack's heart. He wondered if he should have invited his friend to take part in such a dangerous exercise.

When they reached the front door of the house its tenants were already streaming out, no doubt heading to one of the public air raid shelters where, hopefully, they would be protected in the event a bomb fell nearby. Already, searchlights were springing up to fire harsh beams of light towards the stars, questing for Nazi aircraft.

The outflow of residents from the flats meant that Jack and his companions couldn't enter. Not that they needed to, because he saw a familiar face emerge.

Rowena's head was heavily bandaged. The tightness of her expression suggested her wounded scalp still hurt. Nevertheless, her eyes immediately widened in surprise when she saw who stood just outside the door.

"Jack? What on Earth are you doing here?"

"I need to speak to you."

"Why? And who are these men?"

"This is Mr Holmes. That's my friend, Bill Tulley."

From a nearby park came the first loud bangs as the big guns fired shells into the sky. Balls of fire, meteors in reverse, or so it looked, streamed upward. Jack couldn't see any aircraft; although they might have been so high that they were invisible from the ground.

Holmes stepped forward. "We must continue this

conversation later. I fear we're about to receive some rather unwelcome visitors."

Rowena stared at the man in astonishment. Jack suspected she might comment on Homes' quaint Victorian mode of speech.

However, she simply nodded sharply. "We'll make for the underground station. It's a lot deeper than the public shelters."

"Very well," Holmes said.

A movement out of the corner of Jack's eye attracted his attention. An elderly lady bundled in a heavy black coat that reached the ground limped with painful difficulty through the door. She carried a cage in which a budgie whistled frantically as if sensing approaching danger.

"I'll end up dying in the street," she declared. "Why I didn't stay cosy at home, I'll never know. Pippy will catch his death in this weather.

The bird trilled loudly.

Jack turned to Rowena. "Go on ahead with Bill and Mr Holmes. I'll help the lady to the shelter."

Rowena and Bill nodded, and hurried along the avenue in the direction of the station.

However, Holmes shook his head. "Jack, I'll help you. Take the lady's arm. I'll carry our feathered friend."

"Careful with Pippy," she ordered sharply. "He doesn't care for bouncing."

Jack helped the lady walk, although progress was very slow. She seemed in a great deal of pain from her leg. Holmes carried the cage. Meanwhile, Pippy whistled evermore frantically.

They crossed the avenue to a structure consisting mainly of sandbags. An ARP man in a white helmet stood at the top of half a dozen steps that led down to a door.

"Only room for one," he called. "Rammed to the rafters in there."

"That's all right," said Jack. "Only the lady is staying."

"And the bird," Holmes added, handing the cage to the ARP man.

The ARP man jerked his thumb at the sky. "You need to step lively and find cover. They'll soon be here, the Jerry bastards."

Another volley of shells thundered from guns in the park.

Within seconds, the lady, the ARP man, and the bird, were safely in the crowded shelter. The heavy timber door swung shut with a bang. Bolts being drawn shut sounded from the other side.

"It'll only take a couple of minutes to reach the station," Jack said. "But we best hurry."

They walked briskly back along the avenue toward the crossroads. That's when the first bombs began to fall.

12. Blitzed

Searchlights projected beams of brilliant light to prowl the sky in search of the enemy. Anti-aircraft guns sent echoing bangs across the city. Artillery shells rose into the night sky – from this distance, appearing as tiny pearls of light that blossomed into fire as they detonated a mile above the Earth. They did not stop the attack.

Jack heard the piercing scream of falling bombs as he and Holmes rushed along the avenue. The first bombs fell into the next street with a sound that went beyond mere noise. Jack didn't so much as hear the eruptions as feel their shockwave punch his gut. A series of flashes lit the tree branches above him. More bombs were falling all around them.

Holmes actually managed an impressive sprint. Jack pounded along the pavement alongside him.

Holmes shouted, "Keep under the trees as much as you can. They'll help shield us from debris."

Good advice, because already bricks, flung into the air by the explosions, rained down. A section of cast iron rainwater pipe struck the road to embed itself there, end first, a metal javelin as near as damn it. A bomb landed in the back garden of a nearby house. Instantly all the glass in the front of the building shot out across the front lawn, carried by the blast.

"If we'd been caught by the glass..." Holmes panted. "It would have stripped the skin from our bones."

Even as he finished the sentence a flurry of thuds came from all around them. Jack saw slim metal cylinders as long as his forearm hitting the ground.

"Incendiaries," he shouted as they ran.

These incendiary devices, dropped by enemy aircraft, didn't explode on impact. Instead, within seconds, they began to burn with a blue light of such intensity that to look at one of those flaming objects would dazzle the eyes to the point of temporary blindness. These little bombs were designed to punch through roof tiles. There the weapons would lie in attics as their magnesium core burnt at a temperature of more than three thousand degrees centigrade, hot enough to immediately set fire to the timberwork inside the roof.

Acrid fumes from the blazing incendiaries stung the back of Jack's throat. His eyes watered. Another high-explosive bomb struck the end of the avenue. The blast made Holmes stagger. Jack caught him before he fell onto a shimmering carpet of broken glass.

Jack shouted above the raging thunder of exploding bombs, "We can't stay out in this! We'll be killed."

Holmes pointed at a large building to their right. A door yawned open. "In there. We'll take cover!"

A sign by the door stated: EMERGENCY HQ.

Jack followed Holmes into a large entrance hall where a broad staircase curved up to the next floor. ARP men and women in nurses' uniforms hurried on urgent errands. More men and women in civilian clothes sat at tables with clipboards, directing emergency workers to parts of the city where the air raid had struck.

A man ran downstairs, shouting, "Take cover in the basement. Down those stairs by the door. Hurry!"

Jack and Holmes were closest to the open door. A narrow staircase led downward to a vault lit by oil lanterns. They clattered down the steps. Behind them, men and women filed through the shelter doorway.

Jack never even heard the bomb that smashed its way into the heart of the building. One second he ran down the steps. The next, the entire basement seemed to spin with a furious speed. A flash of light seared his eyes then he found himself falling into total darkness.

13. The Same as Them, Blessedly So

Jack Crofton opened his eyes. He realised he lay on a stone floor. A white mist filled the basement. Scents of wood smoke tickled his nose. Silence… Absolute silence. His ears felt as if they'd been packed hard with cotton wool; a peculiarly unpleasant sensation. He lay on his stomach, head to one side, with his left ear resting against cold stone. A small shard of brick lay just next to his fingers – they, too, rested on the floor. He picked up the piece of brick, tapped it on the stone slab. He couldn't hear the sound of tapping. He tried again. Harder. Nothing.

He thought: *I've been deafened by the explosion.*

What's more, the blast had knocked the strength out of him. He couldn't move – couldn't even raise his head. He blinked as the mist became less dense. *Dust… Has to be dust in the air causing the mist.* He understood that. Also he understood that a huge bomb had struck the building, hurling him down the steps into the basement. A single oil lantern, hanging from a wall hook, remained alight.

Jack couldn't see Holmes. However, he realised he wasn't alone down here. As the mist gradually thinned he made out figures lying on the floor. These were men and women of the Emergency HQ staff. Some wore uniforms, others were in civilian clothes. However, they had one factor in common. They were all dead. All mutilated. All ripped apart by the explosion. And all the bodies looked as if they'd been immersed in a vat of blood. They lay there – what remained of their jackets and skirts soaking wet. Skin glistened, bright red. Most were missing arms and legs. Others suffered decapitation.

By sheer chance, Jack had been first into the stairwell; his life probably spared by people crowding onto the steps behind him. Their bodies had shielded him as they absorbed the worst of the blast.

"One day I shall write poetry about this," he murmured. Then shuddered with revulsion at saying such a thing. He licked his lips. They were gritty. Tasted of dust. His back ached. The palm of his hand that he could see in front of him was grazed from the fall.

With an effort he managed to lift the hand. Yet moving his arm seemed to have the same power as waving a magic wand. The corpses began to move. All in a gentle, slow way. They didn't rise to their feet. This was no miraculous resurrection by a forgiving Christ. Even though they still lay on the floor they managed to shuffle and squirm and slide their way toward him. Slowly... slowly... the open wounds in their bodies parted then closed like the full red lips of a lover, approaching to bestow tender kisses. The wounds made a wet sucking sound as they moved.

I can hear again... I don't want to hear... Not this. Not those kissing, sucking noises of wounds... snicking open then closing with a squelch.

Jack tried to stand. He could, however, barely raise his head from the cold slab under his ear. The wriggling corpses got closer. Bodies moving with a slow, undulating motion. Those with heads seemed to drag those lifeless balls of flesh and bone as an afterthought. If there were eyes still in the sockets, they were dull – the whites covered with red speckles. The faces: bland, expressionless. The dead – lifeless and broken-backed. Yet moving, always moving.

When the squirming dead reached him they slowly, wearily, draped their arms over his body. Sometimes, just a shortened section of arm that terminated in shredded muscle and the pulpy yellow worms of exposed arteries. The corpses gently held Jack as if they adored him. What remained of faces on shattered skulls scraped across the floor closer and closer until they were pressed against his chest.

A dead beauty, with wide eyes and crimson lips, gazed fondly at Jack. Softly, she murmured, "It's because I love you that I want you to be the same as them."

All the other corpses, that still possessed mouths, began to whisper the same words.

"It's because I love you that I want you to be the same as them."

Then a familiar voice came from nearby. "Jack, they aren't speaking to you. That which is inside of you is speaking through them."

"Holmes? Where are you?"

"Here I am, my friend. Let me remove you from your adoring disciples."

Jack saw a pair of hands pull the corpses away that had fastened themselves to him. A *post mortem* cuddle.

Holmes spoke gently, "Endeavour to stand, old boy. That's it. Keep trying. You don't look in any way damaged physically. It's probably just shock."

"The bomb..."

"Yes, a veritable behemoth. The blast collapsed the building above us. There... look, you're standing by yourself."

"I am?"

The detonation had left him so disorientated he didn't realise he'd managed to balance himself on his own two feet.

Dead hands clutched at his ankles. Jack wanted to kick them away, but that sad, torn mass of humanity were husbands, wives, fathers, mothers... The deceased's loved ones wouldn't know about the deaths for hours, or even days. Children would glance toward the front doors of their homes when hearing footsteps;

they'd smile, expecting Mum or Dad to step through the door to embrace them.

"Never again," Jack murmured.

Holmes glanced at Jack in a kindly way as he guided him further back into the basement. Holmes scooped a lantern from its wall hook to the light the way. A moment later, he indicated that Jack should enter a room off the main cellar, then closed the door behind them before dragging a heavy filing cabinet across the doorway to block the way in.

Holmes sighed. "I rather think we should not accept any visitors for the time being."

"I made them come back to life, didn't I? Or rather this thing inside my head did... just as it had the power to take over the flying of the V1."

"Yes, the Death Drive literally had the power to drive the dead."

"Thank God, they can't get in here." Jack glanced around the windowless room. "But then we can't get out. And what if the ruins up there are burning?"

"I think we are quite safe. No smoke is being drawn down here; at least not dangerously so."

"We can't stay in the basement forever."

"Nor shall we. Although I fear we will have to, as the young say nowadays, 'sit it out' until rescuers clear rubble from the stairwell."

Jack sat down on a wooden crate. "Did you see those things? The way they touched me."

"I especially noticed what they told you. 'It's because I love you that I want you to be the same as them'."

"Meaning?"

Holmes placed his hands together, finger tips touching; a habit Jack now associated with the man sinking deep into his own thoughts. "That element of your mind wishes to destroy you out of love, not hate. That much is clear to me."

"How can killing me be an act of love?"

Holmes settled down on a stack of newspapers tied up with string. "Our bodies respond to external stimuli. We shiver when we are cold. Perspire when hot. If you cross your legs and tap your knee in the right place your foot kicks forward. Those are reflex actions that we cannot control. There is a segment of your mind that is reacting automatically to some powerful stimulus. It does not choose to do so, any more than you can choose not to shiver if cold, or sneeze if you inhale dust." He nodded. "That segment inside your head is striving to protect you from suffering any more pain in the only way it knows how."

"By making people I care about suffer? Remember – Rowena's accident with the drill. Didn't some part of me cause her hair to be caught by the drill-bit?"

"Yes, I believe the thing inside of you caused that to happen."

"Why?"

"To increase your self-loathing, thus lowering your resistance to the Death Drive that grows increasingly powerful inside of you. Your remorse, which is becoming self-hatred, is making your Death Drive ever more potent."

"How do you know all this?"

"I am a detective by nature. I delve into the workings of the human mind, analysing those inner psychological forces that drive a human being to act in a certain way. Or, indeed, refrain from acting in a certain way. Consequently, I have studied those great investigators of the human condition - Jung, Freud and Adler." Holmes stood up to slowly pace back and forth in the little subterranean room: the image of a professor lecturing students. "Picture the human skull as a zoo that contains animals that are varied in appearance and possess radically different abilities. I've spoken before about the Freudian concept of Eros, the instinct that urges us to live – and to survive in the direst of circumstances, and still crave to bring more children into the world. And I've told you about the Death Drive; the opposite side of the coin to Eros."

As Holmes spoke, the 'thump' of falling bombs faded away. Jack couldn't hear the air-raid sirens, nor any other sound from outside as he listened to the gentle, melodic voice of the man who called himself Sherlock Holmes. The man's claim to be the great detective no longer seemed so impossibly strange. After all, just moments ago, Nazi aeroplanes had cascaded tons of high explosive down onto the city. Houses blazed, roads cratered, gas mains fractured. Hundreds of civilians would be lying dead. This vile reality of wartime was much stranger than a man claiming to be a fictional character.

Hitler's neurotic lust for power at any cost had reached out from his lair in Germany to enter the homes of the Mr Smiths and Mrs Browns, and all those ordinary people whose own lives rode currents of love for their own family. They had no desire to transform nations, or build new world orders, or worship hate beneath the crooked cross. They were people who merely wanted to earn their living, pay domestic bills and spend happy times with family and friends. Now they were blood and rags, and little more. Jack knew that compared with the awful tragedy of mass killings his private war with his own personal monster that existed in a tiny smudge of brain tissue inside his cranium was trivial. Absolutely unimportant alongside a little child crying for its mother in a burning bedroom. And yet... and yet...

Jack finally understood. Fear coupled with nothing less than cold despair oozed downward through the core of his spine, before spreading out through his stomach. He shivered. "Mr Holmes," he said, "am I making this war happen?"

"You are beginning to realise the truth, aren't you?"

"I think so."

"Throughout history, there are many legends that reflect the Death Drive. In ancient Greece, Thanatos was the image of Death in human form. There, the personification of Death was often depicted as a youth who had wings growing from his back. In early Christian mythology many people were seduced by the notion of *Cupio Dissolvi* – Latin for 'I wish to be dissolved'. *Cupio Dissolvi* is an overwhelming desire to leave what believers considered to be a miserable life on earth for the eternal joy of heaven. Others used the term in a more visceral, aggressive way to describe the lust for self-destruction."

"Mr Holmes, am I to blame for the war?"

"To say 'yes' would fuel your remorse, and your self-hatred, which would make your Death Drive even more powerful."

Jack stood up and slammed his fist against the barricaded door. "Did I cause what happened out there?"

A faint scraping sound came, as if hands stroked the woodwork on the other side. Jack pictured those hands that would be wet with blood and shuddered.

Holmes shook his head; those eyes, which were so wise and compassionate, fixing on Jack. "Not solely you. Not you alone."

"There are more like me with... with this Death Drive running amok?"

"Oh, yes. Millions and millions. Individually, the Death Drive is relatively weak. Collectively, its energy, multiplied a million fold, creates an irresistible road to war and mass destruction."

"Surely, that is an example of evolution going wrong? If millions of human beings are gripped by an urge to kill themselves, then aren't we heading toward extinction?"

"On the contrary. In fact, evolution has developed a powerful means to safeguard a species when overpopulation occurs and animals of the same species have to compete for a limited source of food. Then, in order to ensure that at least some animals survive, they begin exterminating each other – not for food, but just to kill. Or they might destroy themselves by stopping eating. If there are too many rats living in a barn they will do the same. Humans do this, too. If you've been on an overcrowded bus, where people are crammed together, you might become flustered, hot and short of breath: that is the self-murder instinct rising inside of you, trying to take control, because that instinctive nature within ourselves interprets an over-crowded bus as dangerous over-population. Naturalists call this Lemming Fever."

"Then if this instinctive compulsion for a thinning-out of human beings is so widespread then there's no hope for me... or for anyone?"

"We must always hope, Jack. No matter how desperate our circumstances might be. Therefore, imagine that people's minds are linked together like telephones to a network of wires. If I can only bring your own drive toward self-destruction under control then your mind might well send out a signal to all those other minds similarly affected, which may switch off the collective desire for mass-suicide."

"Telepathy?"

"Or something more organic. Certain animals, when feeling threatened, can give off a scent that causes other creatures of their own kind to become suddenly more aggressive. Perhaps some of us literally give off a Death Wish odour, yet it is so subtle that this morbid fragrance evades our sense of smell."

Jack glanced down at the floor. Blood trickled from beneath the woodwork of the door. He pictured the slaughterhouse that was the basement. All those corpses. Blood congealing now. Thicker. Darker.

Holmes pulled a sheet of paper from his coat. "Today, I visited the library and read a book, *Yorkshire Talkie & Verse*."

Jack looked at him in surprise. "That's my book."

"How better to look into a man's mind? Reading what you have written is most instructive."

"And?"

"I have made certain deductions."

"By reading my poetry?"

"Indeed. Most of your verses focus on death."

"A subject tackled by every poet."

"Yet you write of death being triumphant in some poems, and being desirable in others."

"You want to psychoanalyse me through my poetry?" Jack shook his head. "Even if you do, what will that achieve? How will your analysis stop me being driven to kill myself? Because that's what this bloody, odious Death Drive is trying to do, isn't it?"

Holmes unfolded the paper. "I copied these lines from one of your poems in the book. Please listen: *Then dying must grant perfection. Like life nails joy to sorrow, so the embracing grave will be my Venus.*"

"That was the first poem I had published."

"And it reveals that you carry a secret."

"What of it?" Jack felt shivery now. Defensive. Wishing to escape from this tomb of a place that adjoined what so closely resembled a bloody slaughterhouse beyond the door.

Holmes spoke softly. "Jack. There's a secret that you never reveal to anyone."

Jack's face became hot. "Did your detective's eye uncover that secret in my poetry?"

"I care about you, Jack. I want to help."

"How can you help?" Jack heard anger driving his voice. "You say you are Sherlock Holmes. The great sleuth. The famous detective. What if you're tricking me? How can I believe you are who you say you are?"

"I investigated many cases successfully."

"The Giant Rat of Sumatra?"

"Yes."

"That isn't a complete Sherlock Holmes case. It's only mentioned in one of the stories. You are a fraud." Jack shoved the man back against the wall. Holmes's mouth twisted in pain. "When I get out of here I'm going to report you to the police. You're a conman!"

Holmes took a deep breath, trying to quell the agony in his back. "Conan Doyle never wrote the case up into a story – that's true. But I investigated the Giant Rat of Sumatra. I solved the crime."

Jack sneered. "A man-eating rat, I suppose. 'Grab your revolver, Watson. The game is afoot. Gadzooks. Where's my deerstalker and magnifying glass?'." Jack gave a bitter laugh. "You sicken me."

Holmes spoke with an understated dignity. "The Giant Rat of Sumatra wasn't an animal. The phrase was a euphemism for a profit-sharing scheme amongst colonialist men who threw people

84

out of their homes in the Sumatran hills in order to mine for silver. They bribed officials, murdered protestors, and poisoned farmland through the use of toxic chemicals employed in the process of extracting silver from the ore. The Giant Rat was indeed a formidable rodent, gnawing through innocent lives, but ultimately the creature consisted of a body of greedy men." Holmes took a step forward and turned his face in such a way as if to invite Jack to hit him. "You have a choice, sir. You can strike me down, or you can tell me that secret which you've kept locked inside of you since childhood."

Jack ran his fingers through his hair, bewildered, angry, frustrated. "I don't know what you want to hear. I can't think of anything other than I was an only child growing up in a Yorkshire village. My father's a coal miner. My mother worked at a textile mill."

"There is something. The ghost of that memory haunts your work."

Jack paced the room. He could taste the blood that had been spilt here in the basement. Its fumes must be stealing under the door to touch his tongue. He thought of his bedroom door at home.

Holmes said, "Tell me your childhood memories. Don't rank them in importance. Just speak them aloud as they come."

"I liked going to the cinema," he said. "When I was seven or eight I cut photographs of film stars out of magazines and covered my bedroom door with them. From top to bottom. They even brushed the carpet at the bottom there were so many."

"Indeed." Holmes fixed those deep-set eyes on him. "Photos all the way down the door."

"Yes."

"Rather odd, isn't it? Fixing photographs to the bottom of the door, so they hung down over the gap and brushed against the floor. Did they not catch and tear?"

"Sometimes."

"What did you do?"

"Replaced the torn ones with other photos."

"In order to block off the gap between the bottom of the door and the carpet."

"Yes." Jack stopped pacing. Waves of heat and cold ran through him. Suddenly, he felt queasy, panicky, as if he'd seen something that frightened him. Or that was an object of disgust.

Holmes spoke gently yet persistently, cutting down through layers of memory to the truth. "Why did you feel compelled to block the gap between the door and the carpet?"

Jack swallowed. "To stop my brother looking in at me under the door."

"He used to do that a lot?"

"Yes... I remember seeing his two eyes there in the gap. He stared at me when I lay in bed." He shuddered. "I can picture them now. A pair of eyes, just staring."

"Did you tell him to stop?"

"How could I? My brother died before I was born."

"Ah."

"As I said, I was only eight or so. I must have dreamt about the eyes."

"Tell me about your brother."

"Not much to tell." Jack shivered as if an ice cold hand touched the back of his neck. "He died when he was three – that was five years before I was born. My mother and father never mentioned him. I heard about him from a cousin. My brother's name was George. Until now, I hadn't thought about George in years. In fact, I'd forgotten all about him."

"His death must have left a void in your parents' lives."

"My mother always baked a big cake on his birthday. I didn't realise that it was his birthday cake until years later. Oh, I'd still eat the cake to please my mother. After that, I'd go out into the garden to be sick." The words loosened inside Jack, flowing faster and faster from his mouth. "My mother used to kiss George's photograph every night. She'd tell him how much she loved him. She did it secretly. At least she believed nobody saw her. I did –

lots of times. Parents don't realise that their children spy on them and eavesdrop. We learn our mother's and father's secrets, don't we? Then we brood on them, worry about them, but we can't say anything because we're afraid our parents will be angry with us for snooping."

"What are your feelings toward your brother, George?"

Jack's face burned with both shame and fury. "I hate him. I really hate him! My mother loves him more than me – how can I compete with a perfect son who died, and who will never disappoint his parents? Because I'm a disappointment to my father. He's ashamed to tell his pals down the pub that his only son's a poet."

Holmes held up the sheet of paper where he'd copied down lines from Jack's book. "All these poems of yours – they celebrate death, don't they? They reveal that you adore the notion of being dead. Death made your brother perfect in your mother's eyes." Holmes rested his hand on Jack's arm. "And now it's time to stop writing love letters to Death."

A fist pounded on the other side of the door. The sound was shockingly loud. Instantly, Jack's gaze locked onto the gap beneath the door, expecting to see a pair of big, shining eyes staring at him.

He saw nothing.

A voice bellowed, "Hello! Anyone in there?"

Holmes called back. "Yes. I'll free the door." He pushed aside the filing cabinet.

The door swung open to reveal men with torches. Some were police, others firemen.

A police sergeant beckoned them. "This way, gents. We've cleared the rubble. Mind how you go. Careful where you put your feet. We're evacuating the living first."

Jack Crofton followed Holmes, picking a route through the grisly maze. His foot slipped on something wet. He didn't look down. Even so, he pictured an eye – a large, shining eye beneath the sole of his shoe.

14. The Monster, the Bringer of Death. Mercifully and Lovingly So

Jack left the remains of the building at a run. Holmes trailed behind him now, his strength flagging. The man's reserves of nervous energy had almost run dry. His face had become increasingly gaunt in recent hours. The face more skull-like. In the gloom, his eyes were mere tiny sparks of light, glinting from the deep sockets in his face.

Jack called back over his shoulder: "All being well, Rowena and Bill are down on the Tube platforms; that'll be the safest place."

"You go on ahead." Holmes' voice turned whispery as exhaustion took hold. "Find them."

"I'm not leaving you behind." Jack slowed his pace, even so he felt a powerful urge to run at full-speed to the station. Right now, he longed to see Rowena and Bill's faces and know that they were alright.

Behind them stood a heap of rubble that had once been the Emergency HQ. There they'd sheltered in the basement. A massive bomb had devastated the place. Elsewhere in the street, homes and shops didn't possess a single unbroken pane of glass between them: shattered windows, roofs stripped of tiles. Debris crunched under their feet. In every direction, flames roses from burning houses. The Nazi air raid had been colossally destructive.

And yet, for all that devastation of the city, the night had become strangely muted. Their footsteps were softly muffled thuds as they hurried across a carpet of soil thrown out of a garden by a bomb. Jack glimpsed a deep crater, which was slowly being filled with water from a broken water main. The liquid formed a shining mirror that reflected the stars. All the anti-aircraft guns had fallen silent now that the enemy had deserted the sky. Most people were still taking cover in the shelters, however, in case another Nazi squadron arrived to shatter more homes and tear apart lives.

Jack made out the distinctive symbol of the London Underground sign on the station wall. No doubt hundreds of people would be sheltering in the subterranean passageways and rail-side platforms.

His footsteps quickened. Holmes matched his pace: the man's features, a tight mask of effort as he drew on his last reserves of strength. A church clock rang twice – two in the morning. Frost whitened bricks in the street that had been flung there by fierce explosions. They skirted another crater in the road. A dead face peeked out from pulverised asphalt; the jaws denuded of skin.

A mouth without lips sighed, "Jack, because I love you…"

Jack hurried by, not wanting to hear what the head would say to him.

Holmes spoke with a fierce intensity: "Jack. Your moment of crisis is approaching. The creature inside your brain will be at its strongest now. Prepare yourself. Soon you will have to fight for your life."

"How can I fight that thing? After all, it'll be the same as trying to fight a nightmare – it's impossible."

"I'll be there to help. Ultimately, however, you must use your own intuition and your own intelligence. Those are your weapons."

Jack nodded before making his way toward the station. A flat-backed truck passed along the road in front of them. A fresh harvest of London dead formed a high mound on the back. More victims of Hitler's evil ambition.

Jack moved faster, eyes fixed on the station. "Thank goodness. The building hasn't been hit."

However, when he was still thirty yards, or so, from the station entrance he heard a woman's voice cry out – a loud cry, combining fear and the determination to overcome some brutal crisis: "Jack… Jack! We're over here!"

He turned toward the direction of the voice. "Rowena?"

The woman stood at the entrance of a narrow street, flanked by high walls at either side. Her eyes blazed from the gloom; her face, a pale disk, and the bandage bound around the top of her head was as white as a skull freshly stripped of its skin.

Jack immediately ran toward her. "Where's Bill?"

"He's down there." She glanced back along the narrow lane. "One of the explosions threw him against a wall. He's hurt his leg. He can't walk."

Rowena led the way at a run. They'd covered perhaps fifty paces when the lane came to a dead end, blocked by rubble from what appeared to be a bombed-out warehouse. A mound of bricks, as high as a house, filled the lane from one side to the other. Jutting vertically from debris to Jack's right, a metal tube, perhaps five feet long. A pillar of flame shot upward by a good ten feet from the tip of the tube, burning brightly with a hissing sound. Clearly, a pipe that had once fed the warehouse with gas. Now broken and ignited by a bomb, escaping gas illuminated the surrounding area with a vivid, blueish light.

Bill lay in the middle of the lane. Rowena had placed her rolled-up coat beneath his head as a pillow, so his head wouldn't rest on filth and broken glass.

Bill's face was streaked with dirt and twisted with pain, yet he managed to smile when he saw Jack.

"We took the wrong way, Jack," he grunted. "Bloody whopper must've hit that place just before we got here. Then another blast from over yonder knocked me clean off my feet."

Jack said, "How's the leg?"

"Busted."

"Can you walk at all?"

"Not a chance."

"I'll carry you."

"You'll never shift me, mate. I'm heavy as a hippo."

Jack knelt beside his friend, feeling sharp fragments of brick dig into his knees. "Don't worry. We'll get you to hospital, even if I have to push you there in a wheelbarrow."

"That's the way, Jack. Deliver me to hospital in style."

Jack glanced at Rowena. "Are you hurt?"

"I'm fine. We were following a sign to a public shelter until we saw that." She nodded at the barrier of rubble. "Before we could go back the other way a bomb fell into the railway cutting at the other side of the wall. That's when Jack broke his leg."

Holmes patted her on the shoulder. "Don't worry, my dear. I'll go back to the road. There's bound to be an ambulance along soon. I'll make them stop."

Jack could feel the tingling heat from the burning gas. The light turned Bill's face a ghostly blue. His friend's eyes seemed to look inside himself, staring at the pain that gnawed at his shattered leg.

Holmes knelt to examine Bill. "No sign of concussion, no lacerations. With luck, the shinbone suffered a clean break. He'll be back on his feet in a month or so."

Jack smiled down at his friend. "Hear that, Jack. You'll soon be chipping away at your sculptures in no time."

Holmes stood up. "I'll go find an ambulance, or a police car. The sooner we…" His voice faded as he noticed something that alarmed him. "Rowena?"

Jack looked up at the woman. Her pale skin turned suddenly paler, her face now resembled a skull mask in that light cast by the burning gas. "That's not possible, is it?" She pointed along the lane. "Look at him."

Jack rose to his feet. The expression of shock on her face sent a flurry of icy shivers across his skin. His gaze followed the direction of her pointing finger. At the end of the lane, some fifty paces away, was a figure in silhouette. The figure stood with its feet apart, facing in the direction of Jack and his companions. What was so striking about the new arrival was the object it held. The stranger's left hand gripped the tail fin of a bomb. The bomb, itself, stood on end, its nose resting on the ground. Jack clearly saw the vertical cylinder reaching as high as the figure's waist.

Holmes shouted, "You there. Gently set the bomb down on its side then move away as quickly as you can."

"Dear God," Rowena hissed. "Why on Earth has he picked up an unexploded bomb?"

"Looks like a two-hundred pounder to me," Jack murmured. "Just hope that it's dud."

Holmes' expression was grim. "If that fellow drops the thing and it goes off?"

Rowena shuddered. "We wouldn't stand a chance."

Bill heaved himself up onto one elbow in order to see for himself what was happening. "He doesn't look right to me… what's wrong with his body?"

The figure moved, slowly placing one foot in front of the other. The heavy cylinder, packed with high explosive, made a grating sound against the asphalt. The figure steadily approached, dragging the bomb.

Jack knew with agonizing clarity that what scraped against the ground was the brass nipple that was designed to crumple inward on impact to trigger the detonation charge, which in turn would make the bomb explode.

Holmes shouted, "Hey, you there. Don't come any nearer."

The figure continued walking, getting closer and closer, dragging the lethal weapon – one that had the power to flatten a dozen houses.

Rowena gripped Jack's arm. "What does he want?"

"Me," Jack murmured.

"Oh, dear Lord." The sight before her was so shocking her

fingers clenched with a force that must have left bruises on Jack's forearm. "That poor man."

Holmes voice came with the sharpness of a whip snapping the air. "That *poor man* is dead."

"His body…" Rowena leaned against Jack for support. "He must have caught the full blast of an explosion."

"And now he's found a UXB… an unexploded bomb. He's bringing something here that will finish the job once and for all."

Rowena's eyes fixed on Jack's face. "What's happening? Do you know him?"

"In a way."

"I don't understand."

"Stay here with Bill and Mr Holmes."

The stranger had entered the field of light thrown by the flaring, hissing gas. Its blue radiance illuminated him in forensic detail. The newcomer was a young man of twenty or so. His feet were bare, his trousers torn. He walked slowly toward them, bare feet crunching down on broken glass, leaving footprints that were a glistening red. The clothes on the top half of his body were gone, probably torn away by the blast. One side of his torso had collapsed, so part of his chest had the inward curving shape of a crescent moon. His face, astonishingly, was unmarked, other than a trickle of blood from one eye. His back, as far as Jack could make out, had suffered injuries that were as terrible as they were bizarre. At either side of the man's back, the skin had been torn away in two large pieces of roughly the same size. They hung down from each shoulder blade, resembling a pair of soft wings that swayed gently as he walked. Gradually, he approached, dragging his gift that promised the start of a long last sleep. The bomb scraped loudly against the ground. Sometimes the nose clanged against a pothole.

Jack pictured the detonator clattering inside its case in the nose. Next time, the jolt might be just hard enough for the bomb to do what its designers intended.

Jack walked forwards to meet the visitor half way. The blue

light flickered, making the scene resemble those jerky images of a silent film. There were no other people about. Apart from the metallic scraping of the bomb across the ground the world seemed uncannily quiet.

The whites of the dead man's open eyes gave off a blue glow as they reflected the gaslight.

"Stop," Jack told the man. "Don't come any closer."

The man did stop. A light breeze made those wings made from his peeled skin flutter.

Holmes had followed Jack. "Remember what I told you about Thanatos," he whispered. "Thanatos is the Greek Spirit of Death shown in human form."

Jack nodded. "A young man with wings."

"This is the personification of the Death Drive inside your head. It has chosen a victim of the blitz that resembles the Greek Spirit of Death. You are being sent a message of absolute clarity that this figure is Death. Your Death."

"It's going to detonate that bomb, isn't it?" Jack recalled earlier in the evening when that monster inside of him took control of the flying bomb and attempted to destroy the house of the inventor. At the last moment, he'd been able to seize control of the V1 and guide it safely away.

Holmes nodded. "Yes. The time of reckoning is at hand."

Jack glanced back at Rowena kneeling beside Bill who lay on the ground. Both watched Jack standing just a dozen paces from the corpse.

"They're trapped in the lane," Jack said. "They'll be killed if that thing detonates the bomb."

Holmes nodded. "I agree, Jack. They won't stand a chance. You, my friend, are our only hope of surviving this."

Jack turned back to the young man with the caved-in ribcage. At the same moment, the corpse moved: powered by the self-destructive forces in Jack's head. A loud scraping noise filled the lane as the figure dragged the cylinder forward.

"Mr Holmes," said Jack, "am I the only one who can control

a V1 in flight, and take over living human beings, and am I the only man capable of making the dead move as if they are alive?"

"I cannot say if you are unique in that ability. All I can be sure of is that an element of your mind has acquired the power to reach beyond your flesh to manipulate matter in the physical world."

The scraping grew louder as the figure walked slowly toward Jack. The expressionless face appeared ghostly blue in the light cast by the gas flame.

The figure stopped a short distance from Jack, then moved its other hand to the bomb so both hands gripped a fin apiece. Muscle stood out from the bare arms as the dead man raised the bomb two feet above the ground. The nose, containing the detonator, was now suspended above the hard surface of the lane.

Jack's heart pounded. Blood thundered through the arteries in his neck. In his mind's eye he pictured the figure slamming the bomb nose-down into the ground, triggering the detonator.

Any second now... Any second...

"Jack." Holmes spoke softly. "Only you can stop him."

Jack gazed into the eyes of the corpse. They glowed bright blue. Each one centred by a hard, black pupil.

Jack glanced at Holmes. "How can I stop him?"

"You, yourself, must decide how."

"It's unlikely I can snatch the bomb from him. That's two hundred pounds of metal and TNT."

Despite what he said, Jack took a step toward the corpse. At that moment, the breeze blew harder. Those two loose sheets of skin hanging from the man's back began to flap in the stream of ice cold air. The corpse didn't move. It didn't have to.

Because Jack heard the sound.

"Ticking," he said to Holmes. "Can you hear it? He's activated the timer. It's become a time bomb."

"Moments, Jack — brief moments, that's all you have to save your friends."

Jack stepped toward the corpse. Its face was expressionless. That figure could have been a statue carved from ice — blue,

Antarctic ice. The flaps of skin fluttered upward, higher than the head of the lifeless youth.

Jack fixed his eyes onto the face.

"I'll go with you," he told the cadaver. "Let my friends live and I will go wherever you want to take me."

That dead thing's mouth moved. "Jack... little brother, Jack."

The features on the corpse blurred then refocussed into that of a three-year-old boy.

Jack's blood ran cold. "Mr Holmes. That's George's face. My brother who died before I was born."

"That's not really your brother."

"But it is. I recognize him from the photograph my mother kept hidden in a drawer."

"Your memory is projecting the image onto the cadaver. Was the bottom third of the photo creased?"

"How did you know that?"

"See the faint line running horizontally across the bottom jaw. You are duplicating the photograph on the cadaver, even down to the crease."

George, or the thing resembling George, spoke in a child's voice: "It's because I love you, Jack, that I want you to be the same as me..." The voice became hollow-sounding – the same as a voice echoing inside a coffin. "Be the same as me, Jack... dead... dead... dead."

The voice stopped. Jack heard the ticking of the clockwork inside the bomb. Tick-tick-tick. The sound became faster, more insistent, promising to burst into a thunderous rage of fire and speeding metal that would shatter bones – killing himself and Holmes and Bill and...

"Rowena."

He felt her hand as she entwined her fingers in his.

She smiled up at him. "We'll face this together."

"I love you."

"I know you do."

Jack turned back to George. "I love you, too. I could feel your presence in our house."

"And it's because I love you, that we shall be the same." George lifted the bomb higher so the cylinder hung from his hands in front of his chest. The ticking grew louder, faster. "Nothing can hurt you in the grave, Jack. You will no longer worry about how to succeed as a poet. Everything is calm beneath that stone which will bear your name. Blissful. A pleasant sleep that never has to end."

Jack suddenly moved. Slipping his fingers free of Rowena's hand, he kissed her on the cheek. After that, he reached out to lightly touch the face of the corpse standing before him. Its flesh was as hard as concrete – the skin so bitterly cold. Jack put his arms around the figure. He embraced Death.

Holmes spoke loudly: "Talk to that element inside of you, Jack. Say what comes into your heart."

The breeze caught the two flaps of skin hanging from the shoulder blades of the corpse. Jack felt their wet touch on his hands as they flapped.

He continued to embrace the body. The ticking of the weapon's mechanism grew louder. The sound echoed from the walls. That metallic heartbeat – no, death-beat – reverberated away into the ground to shake bones lying beneath the Earth far across the world: from ancient tombs in Egypt, with their linen-swathed God kings, to Iron Age skulls in their tumuli, to skinless bones in Medieval crypts, to the still moist flesh in day old graves.

Jack whispered into the cold skin of a dead ear. "I know you are driven to do this because you care about me. But there's no need. Ultimately, I will join you anyway." Jack couldn't be sure how he knew; yet he sensed that Death listened carefully to his words. Then again, how could it not? After all, he spoke to that which existed inside his own head. "My own ending might be a few hours away, or months away. Even if it's seventy years from now, that time will seem to pass by in the blink of an eye. I would like to spend my life with Rowena. And if I am permitted to repent my dedication to writing poetry about a twisted love for morbid subjects I do so now. The only way my mother could deal with her first son dying was to keep on loving him as if he were still alive. I accept that wasn't wrong. Her love was big enough for me, too. I can now accept she adored another child. I should have no monopoly on her love. So, let me be with Rowena. When the time comes in the future for you to claim me in the natural way, then I'll come. Of course, I will."

Jack kissed the side of the corpse's face. The muscles in his lips twitched. His first instinct was to pull back in revulsion. His living mouth against a dead man's ice-cold skin had to be the most horrible thing he'd ever experienced. However, a surge of love overwhelmed disgust. He kissed the face again. This time there was no revulsion. He imagined what would have happened if his brother had lived. How close they would have been. Two soul-mates growing up in a northern town.

He opened his eyes. He found himself supported by Rowena at one side, and Holmes at the other.

"It's all right." Rowena gave a reassuring smile. "You passed out for a while."

"Where is he?"

"He left," said Holmes with a fair measure of satisfaction. "You did it, Jack. You triumphed."

Jack took a deep breath as he now saw what the others had already seen. Climbing a hill in the distance was a solitary figure... Death in human form.

The hill rose from wasteland. There were no buildings nearby. No people.

The figure reached the summit. For a second, the man was sharply revealed as a silhouette against the starry sky. The cylinder rested in his arms like a sleeping baby.

A moment later, the bomb exploded, and the figure was gone.

15. Holmes and Watson

There had been no air raids for a week. Shops in town had put up Christmas trees. Life seemed almost normal again, despite the war raging in Europe and the Far East. As Jack Crofton walked through Fitzrovia, with snowflakes spiralling out of the sky, he heard children practicing Christmas carols in a nearby school.

Followed by the faint strains of *Silent Night,* he crossed the street to where Holmes and Watson lived in their basement flat.

Jack carried a bottle of Famous Grouse whisky. Holmes hadn't asked him to bring one when they'd parted after taking Bill Tulley to hospital in the back of a police car that they'd flagged down. Nevertheless, Jack decided that Holmes, and his friend Doctor Watson, should have payment for the help they'd given him – help that ultimately laid the monster inside his head to rest. Although he knew full well that a pint of Scotch was a hopelessly inadequate reward for saving his life, and the lives of his friends.

Jack descended the snow-covered steps to the flat where he rapped on the door with his knuckles. Feathers of brilliant white snow fell faster. The voices of the children surged, shimmering on the cold, crisp air. After a moment, he knocked again.

Above him, a sash window slid upwards. A woman with grey

hair leaned out to peer down at him in the stairwell.

"Hello?" She smiled pleasantly. "Who are you wanting?"

Jack looked up at her; cold snowflakes tingled on his face and lips. "Good morning. I'm here to see Mr Holmes and Doctor Watson."

"I don't know any Holmes and Watson," she said, puzzled. "Only the two fellers from the films."

"They're the two men who live here. I've visited them before."

"Oh, those two old gents." Her expression turned serious. "The short one took very poorly. I heard it was life and death."

"Is he well now?"

"So, I hear."

Jack knocked on the door again.

The woman said, "No point in doing that."

"Oh?"

"They've gone."

"Do you know where?"

"No, dearie. I heard from my neighbour, a lovely old chap, that they've moved out into the country so the one who was ill can get his strength back in the fresh air. Day before last it was. They didn't have much between them, just a suitcase each." She gave a sympathetic smile. "Sorry. Looks like you've had a wasted trip."

"It doesn't matter. I was just dropping a gift off for them." He raised the bottle to show her.

"They were nice gentlemen," she said as if by way of consolation. "Very polite. Very quiet. Never heard any noise from the pair."

"Did you know that one of them was a famous detective?"

"Oh? I don't think that's right, dear. I heard they were entertainers. You know, a double-act? They used to do little shows at seaside towns before the war."

"They were actors?" Jack stared up at the woman in astonishment.

"So I heard from my neighbour, Mr Palfrey, but then he gets

muddled these days, so maybe he means another couple of gents. Brrr... This cold's getting onto my chest. I'll say good day. Cheerio."

"Cheerio."

She stepped back into the room before sliding the window back down.

Jack gazed at the door to the basement flat for a moment, hoping that the woman had been mistaken, and he'd hear footsteps approaching and then the door opening to reveal that wise and solemn face of Mr Holmes. There was only silence. In fact, the snow had damped down the sounds of London to the extent he couldn't hear the children singing now, nor the sounds of traffic.

For a moment, Jack experienced such a deep sense of loss. Sadness welled up inside of him. He wished he could speak to Holmes again and thank him for the remarkable work he'd done. Snowflakes began to settle on him, turning his shoulders white.

"I can't stand here forever." He gave a sigh of regret.

He began to climb the steps, then paused. For a few seconds he gazed at the whisky in his hand. Making a decision, he went back down the steps again to place the bottle on the ground by the door. An offering of sorts? A symbolic gesture? A message of thanks that Holmes and Watson might hear about one day?

Whatever the reason, he left the bottle of spirit there. An inner voice whispered to him that leaving the token of gratitude was the right thing to do. He realised that he should listen to his instincts more. They offered wise advice.

Quickly, he climbed the steps to the street. His pace was brisk. He felt his spirits rising. He'd arranged to meet Rowena at a café for lunch and he realised how eager he was to see her smiling face.

Jack Crofton, poet, screenwriter and a happier man than he'd ever been before, crossed the square and went out amongst the crowds in Tottenham Court Road. The Christmas lights were coming on in shop windows, children danced and sang on a little stage next to the Methodist Chapel, and, just for a moment, he thought he saw the distinctive figure of Mr Sherlock Holmes, striding along the pavement, weaving through groups of people, before passing deep into that tidal flow of humanity, and finally becoming lost from sight.

About the Author

Simon Clark has written many short stories and novels, including *Blood Crazy, Darkness Demands, Secrets of the Dead* and *The Night of the Triffids*, which continues John Wyndham's classic, *The Day of the Triffids*. *The Night of the Triffids* has also been adapted as a full-cast audio drama by Big Finish and has been broadcast by BBC Radio4Extra.

The year 2014 saw the publication of *Inspector Abberline and the Gods of Rome*, a crime mystery, featuring the real-life Inspector Abberline, who led the hunt for the notorious serial-killer Jack the Ripper, and who went on to become head of Pinkerton National Detective Agency in Europe. Simon has also edited two Sherlock Holmes anthologies for Robinson books, *The Mammoth Book of Sherlock Holmes Abroad* (2015) and *Sherlock Holmes' School for Detection (2017)*.

Simon lives in Yorkshire, England. His website can be found at: www.nailedbytheheart.com

NewCon Press Novellas, Set 2
Simon Clark / Alison Littlewood / Sarah Lotz / Jay Caselberg

Cover art by Vincent Sammy

Case of the Bedevilled Poet ~ His life under threat, poet Jack Crofton flees through the streets of war-torn London. He seeks sanctuary in a pub and falls into company with two elderly gentlemen who claim to be the real Holmes and Watson. Unconvinced but desperate, Jack shares his story, and Holmes agrees to take his case...

Cottingley ~ A century after the world was rocked by news that two young girls had photographed fairies in the sleepy village of Cottingley, we finally learn the true nature of these fey creatures. Correspondence has come to light; a harrowing account written by village resident Lawrence Fairclough that lays bare the fairies' sinister malevolence.

Body in the Woods ~ When an old friend turns up on Claire's doorstep one foul night and begs for her help, she knows she should refuse, but she owes him and, despite her better judgement, finds herself helping to bury something in the woods. Will it stay buried, and can Claire live with the knowledge of what she did that night?

The Wind ~ Having moved to Abbotsford six months ago, Gerry reckons he's getting used to country life and the rural veterinary practice he's taken on. Nothing prepared him, though, for the strange wind that springs up to stir the leaves in unnatural fashion, nor for the strikingly beautiful woman the villagers are so reluctant to talk about...

NewCon Press Novellas, Set 1

Alastair Reynolds – The Iron Tactician
A brand new stand-alone adventure featuring the author's long-running character Merlin. The derelict hulk of an old swallowship found drifting in space draws Merlin into a situation that proves far more complex than he ever anticipated.
Released December 2016

Simon Morden – At the Speed of Light
A tense drama set in the depths of space; the intelligence guiding a human-built ship discovers he may not be alone, forcing him to contend with decisions he was never designed to face.
Released January 2017

Anne Charnock – The Enclave
A new tale set in the same milieu as the author's debut novel *A Calculated Life*". The Enclave: bastion of the free in a corporate, simulant-enhanced world…shortlisted for the 2013 Philip K. Dick Award.
Released February 2017

Neil Williamson – The Memoirist
In a future shaped by omnipresent surveillance, why are so many powerful people determined to wipe the last gig by a faded rock star from the annals of history? What are they afraid of?
Released March 2017

All cover art by Chris Moore

www.newconpress.co.uk

THE ION RAIDER

Ian Whates

The Dark Angels (Volume 2)

Cover art by Jim Burns

The much anticipated follow-up to the Amazon best seller *Pelquin's Comet*.

"A good, unashamed, rip-roaring piece of space opera that hits the spot."
— *Financial Times*

"He's a natural story-teller and works his material with verve, obvious enjoyment, and an effortlessly breezy prose style."
— *The Guardian*

"*Pelquin's Comet* is classic space opera at its finest, a satisfying and enjoyable novel in its own right and an intriguing introduction to a story universe I want to visit again. Thoroughly recommended."
— *SFCrowsnest*

"Whates does a good job playing out the lines of suspense while steadily revealing significant plot points, keeping things character-focused… It's a fast, fun read." — *Speculation*

"You won't go far wrong with this book... you never know, it could be the beginning of something wonderful." — *Booklore*

~

Leesa is determined to find out who is quietly assassinating her old crewmates, the Dark Angels, and stop them before it's her turn to die.

First Solar Bank have sent **Drake** on his most dangerous mission yet, to the isolationist world of Enduril, where nothing is as it seems.

Jen just wanted to be left in peace on her farm, until somebody blew the farm up. She escaped, a fact those responsible will come to regret.

Released May 2017 www.newconpress.co.uk

IMMANION PRESS

Purveyors of Speculative Fiction
www.immanion-press.com

The Lightbearer by Alan Richardson

Michael Horsett parachutes into Occupied France before the D-Day Invasion. He is dropped in the wrong place, miles from the action, badly injured, and totally alone. He falls prey to two Thelemist women who have awaited the Hawk God's coming, attracts a group of First World War veterans who rally to what they imagine is his cause, is hunted by a troop of German Field Police who are desperate to find him, and has a climactic encounter with a mutilated priest who believes that Lucifer Incarnate has arrived...

The Lightbearer is a unique gnostic thriller, dealing with the themes of Light and Darkness, Good and Evil, Matter and Spirit.

"The Lightbearer is another shining example of Alan Richardson's talent as a story-teller. An unusual and gripping war story with more facets than a star sapphire." – Mélusine Draco, author of "Aubry's Dog" and "Black Horse, White Horse". ISBN: 978-1-907737-63-3 £11.99 $18.99

Dark in the Day, Ed. by Storm Constantine & Paul Houghton

Weirdness lurks beyond the margins of the mundane, emerging to dismantle our assumptions of reality. Dark in the Day is an anthology of weird fiction, penned by established writers and also those new to the genre – the latter being authors who are, or were, students of Creative Writing at Staffordshire University, where editor Storm Constantine occasionally delivers guest lectures. Her co-editor, Paul Houghton, is the senior lecturer in Creative Writing at the university.

Contributors include: Martina Bellovičová, J. E. Bryant, Glynis Charlton, Storm Constantine, Louise Coquio, Elizabeth Counihan, Krishan Coupland, Elizabeth Davidson, Siân Davies, Paul Finch, Rosie Garland, Rhys Hughes, Kerry Fender, Andrew Hook, Paul Houghton, Tanith Lee, Tim Pratt, Nicholas Royle, Michael Marshall Smith, Paula Wakefield, Ian Whates and Liz Williams.
ISBN: 978-1-907737-74-9 £11.99, $18.99